ALSO BY ELE FOUNTAIN

Boy 87
Lost
Melt
Fake

ELE FOUNTAIN

PUSHKIN CHILDREN'S

Pushkin Press
Somerset House, Strand
London wc2r 1la

Wild was first published by Pushkin Press in London, 2023

1 3 5 7 9 8 6 4 2

ISBN 13: 978-1-78269-384-0

Designed and typeset by Tetragon, London
Printed and bound by Clays Ltd, Elcograf S.p.A.

www.pushkinpress.com

Contents

For Helena,

and for everyone trying to make a difference

It is only with the heart that one can see rightly; what is essential is invisible to the eye.

ANTOINE DE SAINT-EXUPÉRY
The Little Prince

Broken

An explosion of glass splinters the night air. My ears ring in the silence that follows.

Shiv opens his mouth but the words are swallowed by another shattering sound-burst.

A heavy object presses into my glove. A hand pats me hard on the shoulder. Too hard.

'Get the big one!'

'C'mon! Finish it!'

Shiv laughs a cackling laugh which the others copy.

My back is sweating. Beneath my gloves, my palms are sweating. I don't feel scared though.

'Whoah! He's bottled it!'

'I told you. He's worried what Mummy will think.'

More laughter.

But I've already raised my hand. The brick is flying through the air. The noise that follows has a longer, lower pitch, ending in a few tinkling notes. A jagged hole appears where before, glass reflected the moonlit clouds. I've destroyed a piece of sky.

'Nice!'

'Bullseye!'

There are more pats on my shoulder but this time they feel like a prize. A reward.

Nearby a dog barks. The barking grows closer.

A fat white torch beam slices through the dark, flickering over our clothes.

'Hey!' a voice shouts angrily.

The torchlight wobbles as its bearer runs towards us, followed by a second beam. Two men.

Wordlessly, Shiv and the others grab the handlebars of their bikes and climb on. I have no bike to grab.

Wheels whir as they pedal into the darkness, away from the wobbling torches.

Shiv hangs back. 'Get on!' he growls. 'Do you want to get caught?'

I jump into the saddle and cling to the back of Shiv's hoodie as he pumps the pedals, chasing the others.

A few streets away is an alley. We cut through, to a small car park behind a row of shops.

The shops are all shut. The car park is deserted, except for five figures, panting clouds of vapour into the night air.

'Get a bike,' says the shortest figure, between gasps. 'No one gets caught. You're not going to change that.'

'Jay, leave him. He did all right,' says Shiv.

There are murmurs of approval from the other two.

'Breaking windows is one thing. Is he going to help with the racking?' says Jay. 'We need a load of paint if we're gonna dress that shack.'

I don't know what Jay means. I have literally no idea what he's talking about. I should be panicking. They'll decide I don't belong. They don't need me. But I'm not panicking. I am calm.

Jay seems to notice. So does Shiv.

'Don't be a jerk,' he says casually to Jay. 'He'll help us get the paint. He's in our crew now.'

Jay tuts. 'He's a complete toy. He's just gonna tag everywhere. Then we'll all look like toys. We'll be the "joke" crew.'

'Have you seen his art? Did you look at that stuff in his sketchpad? Each one was a piece.'

The words slot into place.

If we're going to spray inside the old youth club, we'll need a lot of paint. We're going to steal it. If Jay gets his way, I'm going to steal it for them.

Far away, I hear a voice screaming *no no*. But it's too far away to matter.

'I'm in,' I hear myself say.

'In for what?' replies Shiv, head tilted to one side.

'In for whatever you want.'

Shiv nods. The others nod too. Except Jay.

'How do we know he's not just going to rat on us? He knows stuff now. Who we are.'

'We go to the same school, Jay,' snorts Shiv, 'of course he knows who we are.'

'Why is he acting so calm? I mean, we nearly got caught. Maybe that's his plan.'

'C'mon!' the other three groan together. I realize that for some reason they are on my side.

'Maybe you're just jealous, Jay. *Jealous Jay*. That could be your new name,' Shiv adds quietly.

'No, I—'

'We need another rook. Five is better than four. More power. Jake is cool—cool as ice.'

Shiv smiles at the way he sounds.

Slowly, Jay begins to nod too. 'OK.' He stares at me, his face pale orange under the glow of the streetlight. 'We're good. But next week we get the paints. Tuesday.' He raises his eyebrows as if Tuesday is not merely the day before Wednesday, but some kind of threat.

I nod.

I'm in. For anything. Seriously. But if they think I'm brave, they're wrong. To be brave, you need to overcome your fear. But I don't feel fear. I don't feel anything at all.

Spark

I slip my key into the lock. It's way past curfew. The door creaks open. A faint smell of pizza hangs in the air, even though dinner was hours ago. The house has been sleeping since I left. I stand motionless in the hall, listening for signs of life. Silence pushes back.

I pad towards the kitchen, socks slipping on the wooden floor, and pour myself a glass of water. I'm hungry, but I can't be bothered to look for something to eat, so I turn off the light and let my eyes adjust to the gloom. I'm about to head upstairs when I pause. A pale-yellow strip glows beneath Mum's study door. She's not asleep. She's working.

A spark of anger flares in my chest. I should be relieved that she hasn't realized I'm back. That I'm late. That I've been gone for hours. Instead,

I'm annoyed. The glow in my chest burns hotter. Today's happiness, sadness, fear, have finally arrived, repackaged as rage. I feel my heart pumping. I take a step towards the door, then stop. I don't want to talk to her. That's what she wants. She wants me to open up. To share my feelings. If I go in, she'll think she's won. Or that she's making 'progress'. Because it's all about 'tiny steps'. I breathe deeply, then turn and walk away.

The rage ebbs but doesn't disappear. It turns into something bland yet dangerous. Like concrete setting in my veins, it makes me feel tough. Invincible.

Reckless.

Burn

'Jack!'

My eyes flick open.

Mum's silhouette is framed by the doorway, hands on hips.

She's going to give me hell. She knows I missed the curfew.

'I have a meeting at nine. I can't be late. Get yourself ready for school. I'll see you later.'

She steps closer and I realize that she's wearing her blue coat, leather satchel clutched to her chest.

This has nothing to do with the curfew—or with me. Of course. It's about work.

She's giving me a 'look of concern'. I pull the covers over my face.

'We'll do something at the weekend,' she adds, 'maybe watch a movie.'

I cringe at the word 'movie'. She calls them films. Normally. Also, she has no idea what I like. We haven't watched a film together since I was seven. My insides convulse at the thought of sitting on the sofa with her, making small talk about the plot.

The front door clicks shut. I push the covers down to my chin. A flowery scent drifts from the doorway. The only sign that Mum was in the house at all. That I didn't imagine the three seconds of conversation. Can you call it a conversation when one person does all the talking?

I reach for my phone. It's almost eight o' clock. I need to get up.

Last night's rage seems to have made me heavier, well something has. I don't have the energy to lift myself out of bed. Perhaps I really am slowly turning to stone.

I picture arriving at school. Saying hi to my friends. Talking to people. Being nice. Until someone asks about *it*. Because someone always does. Then my day will be over and I'll watch the minutes tick past on the classroom clock until it's time to go home. Back to the flowery scent. If I stay in bed, the flowery scent will receive a call from school that interrupts her meeting, resulting in *a chat*. I have a choice between bad option one, or bad option two.

I get dressed and grab a packet of crisps from the kitchen. My stomach twists with hunger, so I grab another packet—a different flavour. It's important to have a balanced diet.

In the morning, I have a double period, which means less moving around, less chat.

At breaktime, I kick a ball around with the others, then I see Jay over by the fence, talking to Shiv.

The ball thuds against my thigh.

'You're supposed to use your feet,' shouts Dan. He follows my eyes but says nothing.

'I'll be back in a minute.'

'Sure,' he replies.

Shiv looks up as I approach. He doesn't smile, but jerks his chin up, like he's trying to tip something tiny from the back of his head. Jay does the same.

'All right,' says Shiv.

I don't think it's a question.

'Got your bike yet?' asks Jay.

'No. I thought about going to the bike shop on my way home last night, but they were shut. This morning too.'

Shiv snorts. Jay glares at me. Although his expression doesn't really change much from when I first arrived.

'We're going in five,' says Shiv. 'Wanna join? It is Friday after all.'

'Err yeah,' I say.

'He has no clue,' snaps Jay.

'Sure he does. You knew I meant going... elsewhere, leaving school, didn't you, Jack?'

'Sure. Where are we going?'

'Maybe scope some Skylon.'

'Paint,' sighs Jay.

'OK.' I want to look over to Dan, to the others. See if they're waiting for me. Watching. But I don't turn round. I won't give Jay the satisfaction.

'See you round the back of the gym. We'll duck under the fence. Best if we don't go together,' says Shiv.

I nod. I've never skived off school before. There are lots of things I've never done before.

I'm wondering why.

Freeze

Some days, it seems strange that the world keeps on turning, when mine stopped three months ago.

I didn't feel anything. Just shock. Now I don't feel shocked, but there aren't any better words to describe what's happening inside my head. Near the kitchen window lives our tattered blue dictionary. Heavy as a bag of flour. I searched for the right word in there, the thin pages rustling beneath my impatient fingers. There is one which comes close. Nothing obscure; the simplest of all.

Change: to make (someone or something) different

I don't remember a moment when I changed. It wasn't on the actual day. Not the week after either. It wasn't sudden. But I am different.

My feet crunch softly across frosty grass. The

frozen blades yield beneath my trainers, pressed flat in the frozen mud. Cold nips at my nose. Breath puffs round my head like a vaporous scarf. I pull the hood of my sweater down to block the icy wind. Mum hates me doing this. She says only kids in gangs wear their hoods up. I pull it lower.

Ahead, beyond the path, a group of kids kicks a ball around. I don't need to see their faces to know it's Ben and Johannes, Dan and the others. No one moves round the pitch the way Ben does—fast and nimble like a cat, hunting. Although Dan calls him the seal because he also dives whenever anyone tackles him.

I did think about staying in bed. Again. But Dan messaged this morning. Dan's mum knows my mum. They talk. After yesterday—walking off in the playground, missing school in the afternoon—I thought I should come out. Otherwise Dan might mention it to his mum. If Dan mentions it to his mum, she will mention it to mine. It's not a chain of communication I want to activate. Also, it's Saturday.

Johannes sticks his arm up and waves. My legs feel heavier than moments before. I know the only way to make them lighter is to turn and run back the way I came, to keep running and running until

I can't go on. I wonder how far that would be. I wave back.

'Are you going to kick it or are you medicating or something?' Johannes is halfway down the pitch, hands on his hips.

'It's *meditating*, potato-brain,' shouts Ben, even though he's only two metres from Johannes.

Before the Change, I would have laughed. 'Different' me feels nothing. I'm watching myself. I'm a creepy puppet master. I can move my body around, but I can't make it laugh, or smile. Or cry.

The ball rolls slowly towards my feet. I chip it over Dan's head, towards Johannes.

'Nice!' he shouts.

I pull the strings which make a 'thumbs up', because I know that before the Change, I would have felt pleased.

Dan walks beside me. 'I didn't think you were coming today.'

'Why not?' There is a buzz in my stomach, as I wonder whether the strings are beginning to show on 'puppet' me.

'Because you were late!' Dan gives me a sideways smile and shakes his head.

Of course.

'Are you around over the holidays?'

The heavy feeling is almost unbearable. I haven't thought about the holidays. I can't think about the holidays.

'Yeah, I'm around.'

'Let's do something. Maybe we could watch a game on Boxing Day?'

I stop walking. For a split second I stall, as if my brain can't focus on this final sentence and keep me moving too.

'Oh, yeah.' Dan puts his hand to his head. 'Maybe you don't want to because of—'

'No, sounds good,' I say quickly. My legs come back to life and I start jogging towards the centre of the pitch where the others are waiting. If I can't run away, then this is the next best thing—to keep moving. To stay one step ahead of the heaviness.

Pasta

I walk home along empty streets. Dusk is falling. A single star shines in the red-orange sky. Already I feel the temperature dropping. Everyone else seems to be at home, together. Family scenes play out, bathed in yellowish light, framed by curtains and shutters. Little kids watch TV. Someone eats their dinner. A dog jumps up for attention. I wonder what it would be like to live in one of these houses. To live in one of these families. The rooms seem filled with life.

My house is filled with artefacts. With clay pots and carved objects, with maps and papers and thick books, which have crumbling spines and musty pages. The first time Dan came round, he christened our house The Museum. I didn't mind. I thought there were probably worse names he could have come up with. For a brief period back in Year Seven, I was famous. Other kids in my class wanted to visit The Museum, and I would give tours of the house before we watched TV. I had to figure out what the carved objects and pots were used for. My descriptions grew wilder. The jar for storing oil became a receptacle for severed hands. The sundial, a portal to outer space. Mum didn't mind. But then, it's easy to feel relaxed about stuff when you're somewhere else. Especially when 'somewhere else' is thousands of miles away. She would disappear for weeks at a time, to places I'd never heard of. In the beginning, I would search for them on the maps that cluttered her office wall. Maps showing huge islands labelled in strange curly writing, etched on ancient paper, turned golden with age. Sea monsters patrolled the oceans beyond, searching for cracks in the picture-frame glass. They bore no resemblance to the maps I'd seen at school, but I liked looking at them. Behind her desk was a more modern chart of the world, two metres square. Laminated. Round-headed pins punctured the places she'd been to or wanted to visit.

Well, she can't visit them now. I'm the flaw in that particular plan.

I look up and realize I'm almost home. The lifeless feeling drifts around me like a poisonous mist.

I search for the key in my pocket, but my fingers seem to have frozen on the walk back. I didn't notice. As I fumble the key into the lock, the door swings open.

'Hi, darling.'

I retreat in surprise.

A shadow of something flickers across Mum's face, replaced by a smile as she adds, 'Remember me?'

I roll my eyes. I want to push past her and go upstairs, but I know that will make things worse in the long run. She'll give me space for an hour or so, then come to my room and sit on my bed so that we can talk things through. I will even watch a film with her to avoid talking things through.

Which is just as well because seconds later she says, 'Have you chosen a movie? I've bought some popcorn, or at least I think I have. The bags were tiny, so I got six. Do you even like popcorn?'

'Not yet,' I say, answering the movie question, although I realize it sounds as if I expect to like popcorn soon, instead.

'OK, maybe we should have dinner, and you can think about it while you're eating.'

I feel as if I could be in one of Mum's meetings. She has a reputation for 'making things happen'.

I sniff the air, trying to work out what dinner might be. Mum is the worst cook. Everything she makes ends up burnt, runny or both, which shouldn't even be possible.

She interprets my sniff as appreciation.

'Pasta with sauce,' she says proudly.

I plan to use my new standard meal technique for limiting conversation—eating so fast there is barely time for chat, and when Mum does ask a question, I have a mouthful and therefore can't answer. Speaking with your mouth full has never been allowed in our house. A rule which used to annoy me. Before.

'How was school?'

I chew slowly, then murmur, 'Fine.'

'You haven't had Dan round for a while. Have you two fallen out?'

The spark of anger flares again in my chest. We are talking things through, even though nothing's happened. Even though I'm eating my dinner.

'He's fine,' I reply, trying to stay calm.

I feel Mum's eyes on me.

'Perhaps he—'

'I can't talk and think of a film at the same time,' I mutter.

29

'OK,' she answers, using her calm voice. The one reserved for finding lost football socks.

We finish the meal in silence.

Perfect.

Pressure

'Jack, wait.'

I pause in the doorway. The film was good, but I'd seen it before. I had to be sure there was no kissing. Now it's over I just want to lie on my bed.

'Come back for a moment. I want to talk to you.'

Please, no.

I hesitate. I could walk away, but if we talk now, then maybe Mum will leave me alone for the rest of the weekend.

I amble slowly over to an armchair on the far side of the room and sit down. 'For a moment,' I confirm.

'I had a call from school.' She is looking straight at me. 'They said you weren't there for registration yesterday afternoon. That you weren't in your lessons either.'

I should be feeling sick. The old me would be clammy with fear or guilt—or both. Instead, a different sensation surges through me, and I'm not sorry.

I wonder if it shows on my face, because Mum seems to change her tone.

'Darling, next term is really important. You will be deciding what you want to study for the next two years. You'll be making decisions about your future.'

She pauses, waiting for me to speak, but I have nothing to say. The listless feeling has settled, smothering my defiance. Smothering everything.

The person I made plans with, who was here when Mum was away, who helped with my homework. The person who knew what I wanted, before I knew myself. Who knew that I liked salty popcorn but not sweet popcorn. Who never said *we need to talk* because we talked all the time. The person who understood me.

That person has gone.

Now I don't care about my future. Or anything.

'I know it's been hard,' she whispers.

Her words trick me into feeling that he's here. They should have the power to summon him. To make him speak.

I fight the heaviness to stand up. Without a word, I go to my room.

Free

The footsteps get louder, drawing me from my thoughts. I spin round just as Dan grabs me by the shoulder.

'Walk in together?'

'Sure.'

I stuff my hands deeper inside my pockets. I always forget my gloves. Dad used to throw them at my head as I walked out the door. Last winter.

'So tomorrow it's Ben's house. As it's the last week at school, his mum said we can watch the footy on their projector. Saturday, park, then my house for pizza?'

I nod.

'We're going to start a sweepstake for the tournament. The final isn't until May, so we'll need to pace ourselves.'

I kick a small stone lying in my path. Dad and I once discussed sweepstake odds for the World Cup for two hours.

'There's no way I'll buy the new strip though. They put the price up again. If I win the sweepstake then I'll save it to buy next year's.'

The school gates are in sight. Ben is waiting for us.

I never realized how much Dan talks. Everything he says seems hardwired to a memory of Dad.

On the opposite side of the road, a blue car is parked. It doesn't fit in with the other cars ejecting a steady flow of students, rucksacks and instruments. It's lower and shinier, radiating a steady beat which thumps in my chest. The passenger window is wound down, and Jay's arms are resting on the edge, his head halfway inside the car. I hear him laughing.

I wonder what they're talking about. Not football, I bet.

During French, I count down the seconds until breaktime then head to the end of the fence where Shiv and the others hang out. They don't notice me approach.

Shiv spins round. 'Waaay, it's Jacky-boy!'

'Are you going—elsewhere?' I ask.

Shiv laughs. So do the others. 'Elsewhere! I like it. Yes, we are going *elsewhere*. But you should

34

stick around here a bit longer. Until afternoon registration.'

I frown. 'Why?'

'Because you're making us look bad,' says Kai, who has a husky voice, as if he has a permanent sore throat.

He's grinning, but I don't get the joke.

'They don't care about us,' he nods towards the school, 'but if you start skiving, and people see you hanging out with us, we'll be the ones who get harassed.'

'For turning you to the dark side,' adds Shiv. Although I already get the picture. 'Makes life easier for everyone if you do the afternoon reg. Then come and find us in the car park.'

'And you've got a little job to do for us,' smiles Jay. It's not a friendly smile.

'Later,' says Shiv.

They turn their backs on me and carry on talking.

I don't mind though, because all of this is new. Memory free.

Test

I like the buzz of trying not to get caught. I need to focus, which leaves no space for the heaviness to creep in.

After registration, everyone crowds towards the door. Dan and Johannes are near the front, so I hang back. We have maths, but I head towards the gym. In the tide of students, no one pays me any attention. Only the other kids in my class know I have maths, and they're walking in the opposite direction.

The changing rooms are empty. There is a smell of stale sweat. Weird how I never notice it when we change for PE. A single sock lies on the bench. I wonder if that could be the source of the smell. My skin prickles as I imagine the door slamming open behind me and some Year Elevens swarming in for football. So at first I don't notice the boy in front of me, by the lockers.

'What are you doing?' He's in running kit, red-faced and sweating. 'Only the cross-country team has permission to come here during lunch.'

He's taller than me, with broad shoulders. He looks annoyed.

My brain whirrs.

'It's not lunchtime now,' I reach for the sock on the bench, 'and I left this here.'

In the split-second distraction, I walk past, towards the door to the playing fields.

'Hey!' he shouts after me, but his voice lacks the conviction of before. Maybe the smelly sock really was mine. Who would make that kind of thing up?

I don't recognize myself, which feels good. Like a snake shedding an old skin which doesn't fit any more.

I drop the sock in the playground bin and walk towards the fence. Running would look more suspicious, although I doubt anyone is watching.

As I jog along the house-lined streets which lead to the car park, I think about Dan and Johannes stuck in the classroom, copying equations. Being reminded of the 'important choices' lying in wait next year. I almost laugh. I have spent so much time worrying about lessons and homework, all in preparation for those important choices. But three months ago, I learnt that planning for things is pointless. Working hard to make people proud is pointless too. Because the future will do whatever it likes regardless of your plans, and the people you wanted to make proud might just disappear without warning.

I sniff. The cold air is making my eyes water.

The sound of music drifts from the far side of the car park. Shiv and the others are huddled together.

'Come on,' shouts Jay. 'We're solid here. Frozen.'

Shiv laughs. 'I think Jay has a little job he's keen to tell you about. What's up with your face? It's all red and blotchy.'

'Sensitive skin, cold weather,' I say. Shiv laughs again. 'Need a good moisturizer,' I mutter.

'Yeah, well your sensitive face is not known to the guy who owns the art shop,' says Jay, his expression serious. 'So you're gonna be racking some paint for us tomorrow. We'll show you where, and you figure out how.'

'Best scope the paint, then buy a small thing. If you buy, they don't spy. Pick up the paint on your way out,' says Shiv.

'Why don't you take one of your oaty-goodness friends?' adds Kai. 'Those football buddies of yours look way too healthy to do bad things.'

'Are you gonna draw him a picture too?' says Jay. 'No one babysat me on my first job.'

'And you got caught,' says Shiv, 'so best if we do help Jacky-boy. Else none of us gets any paint.'

'Five,' says Jay. 'Get five canisters.'

'You might need a shopping trolley,' grins Shiv.

Take

'If you need to barf, do it that way.' Ben points to the hedge.

'I'm fine. Twenty-four-hour thing.'

This morning, it seemed easiest to tell Dan I'd been ill yesterday afternoon. But he told everyone else, and now Ben is worried I'm going to be sick all over his sitting room.

I tap my pocket to check the money is there. I grabbed some pound coins from Mum's pot of change. Enough to buy a 'small thing'. She won't notice. Not unless the pot of change is somehow related to *work*.

Back in the days of The Museum, my mum was the only parent whose job no one could pronounce. Environmental anthropologist doesn't exactly roll off the tongue. No one knew what it meant either.

Dad said that anthropology is the study of humans, so environmental anthropologists basically cover everything—humans and where they live. His eyes would sparkle when people asked where the 'professor' had jetted off to this time. He never seemed to mind that she only spent half her time in the same country as us. Less than half. I'm not sure I minded very much either. But I had Dad, then.

'Earth to Jack, calling Jack.' I glance up, 'Nachos or crisps?' asks Ben.

'Oh, er, both?'

Our walk to his house clips the edge of town, and part of the high street.

'Actually, I need to pick something up for my mum. From the art shop. Come with me?' I look at Dan.

He hesitates. 'You know Ben will end up buying cheese and onion flavour or something disgusting. We can't let him go alone.'

'Thanks. I'm the one paying for this stuff, remember?' says Ben.

'Let's just stick together. Easier,' says Dan.

We buy snacks, then head to the art supplies shop. Me, Dan, Johannes and Ben.

In the window, bright tubes of paint are piled next to coloured pencil sets and easels.

A bell tinkles as I push the door open. A man with white hair appears at the end of one aisle.

'Let me know if you need any help,' he smiles.

For some reason I'd pictured the owner as younger. Less friendly.

'What are you getting?' asks Ben.

'I need a—Mum needs a notebook. For when she's travelling without wi-fi.' I'm surprised by how convincing I sound.

Ben nods. 'There are some over here. They're quite expensive.'

I zigzag down the aisles towards him, scanning the shelves for cans of Skylon. I know what I'm looking for. I did my research. They're not here. Maybe the old guy doesn't sell it any more.

I can't go back to Shiv empty handed. That's what Jay wants. He'll tell the others I'm not one of them. Perhaps I didn't even try. I slow them down without a bike. This time they might listen.

'This is what she wants.' I reach for a three-pack of lined notepads near Ben's feet. I'm sure they sell them in the supermarket too, but no one says anything. 'I'll pay and meet you outside.'

The others move slowly towards the door, stopping to adjust the arms on the wooden artists' mannequin so she seems to be picking her nose.

I reach in my pocket for the change. As the old man emerges from a room at the back of the shop, I spot the Skylon. It's on a shelf to the right of the till. Less than a metre from where he's now standing. There is no way I could touch one without him seeing. I pull out a few coins, buying myself time to think.

'Do you have any more of those pads? That was the last one on the shelf, but I need two packs.'

'Hmm, let me check in the storeroom,' he smiles.

Once his back is turned, I unzip my bag and reach for the Skylon. I stuff five cans inside. They're smaller than I thought, so I squeeze in a sixth. I'm closing the zip, when he returns, waving something in the air.

'You're in luck! There's a new box. I'll refill the shelf too.'

I hand over my change. 'Thank you.' My mouth is dry. I feel slightly sick. Maybe I am coming down with something after all. I turn to leave. Ben and Johannes are outside talking. Dan is waiting at the end of the aisle. He smiles, but it's a weird, tight kind of smile.

He watched me steal the paint.

Message

There's a note attached to the fridge. I ignore it and open a packet of biscuits lying near the kettle. I eat three, then rip the note from the fridge door.

Jack,

> You might have to get your own dinner tonight.
> There are plenty of things in the freezer.
> Big project going on at the moment.
> Will be home as early as I can.
>
> Love Mum x

I throw it in the bin. Why can't she just message like everyone else? Anyway, I told her I was going to Ben's house.

I sit on the sofa and flick through the channels.

But I'm not really checking what's on. My eyes wander to the empty chair next to the window.

Even though it's only nine p.m. I wander up to bed.

I need to brush my teeth, but the listlessness has returned, pulling me beneath the sheets, whispering *Stay, why bother? What's the point?*

My phone buzzes. There's a message from Shiv.

Success?
I reply **Success.**
Car park after reg tmrw?
I type **Yes.**

I get up to brush my teeth. As I pass the wardrobe, I open the left-hand door a fraction.

The Skylon is stashed at the bottom, beneath some jumpers. Mum will never look there. We have a cleaner now, but she's not exactly going to hoover inside my wardrobe. So I guess they're safe. I want to show them to Shiv tomorrow, but that would mean taking them to school. Instead, I lift the corner of my jumper pile and take a photo.

As I get ready for bed, my phone buzzes again. I snatch it from my desk. But the message isn't from Shiv, it's from Dan. My finger hovers over the icon before I press it.

Left your gloves at Ben's will bring tomorrow.

The spark of anger flares, taking me by surprise.
Dan saw me take the paint. Why hasn't he said
something? Why hasn't he confronted me?
Perhaps he's worried what his mum will think.
Dan worries too much about what people think.

Crew

I don't know what time Mum came home last night. It must have been late. But the next morning, she's sitting by the kitchen table like a sentry, guarding breakfast from latecomers. I feel as if I need to apologize, even though she's the one who's late or somewhere else most of the time.

'Hello, sleepy head.'

I roll my eyes.

'Did you find something to eat?'

'I normally manage.'

'OK.' She makes the second syllable extra-long. 'Only, I couldn't see any plates in the dishwasher.'

'I wasn't hungry.' Which isn't a complete lie. I'd eaten loads of snacks at Ben's house.

'Sorry I was late. I've been asked to help with a big project.'

'I read your note.'

Mum takes a slow breath in and out. 'There's a small indigenous group in a remote area of rainforest.' I hold the chocolate spread and the jam side by side, trying to choose which one I'm in the mood for. 'They're at risk, but no one's been able to contact them.' Maybe honey, actually. 'Some funding has been made available to support conservation efforts in the region.'

I look up. 'Can't you just airdrop some phones, then call them or something?'

Mum pushes back her chair and carries her bowl over to the sink.

'I'll try to be home on time tonight. Then I can cook for both of us.' She hurries to the hall and shouts, 'Bye, darling.'

I put the honey down. I'm not sure I can be bothered to make toast after all. But I know I shouldn't miss another meal.

At school, I keep to myself until afternoon registration, then I head to the gym. This time I wait for five minutes in the toilets next to the changing rooms, to make sure I don't run into tall-runner-guy again. I'm not sure I would be able to dodge past a second time.

As I cross the field to the fence, I realize that my new routine is becoming familiar. The heavy feeling likes familiar. It knows where to find me and creeps back, staying a little longer each time. I might need to do things differently tomorrow.

'Jacky-boy!' Shiv calls from the other side of the car park. He's pleased to see me, and it makes me feel good because he likes the 'Jack' I am now. The Jack who appeared three months ago. Not because I'm the same Jack he's known since infant school.

'So I hear you're the racking prince.' Jay raises his eyebrows without smiling. 'Can the crew have a view?'

I reach for my phone.

'You don't have the real stuff?' says Jay.

'I didn't take it to school.'

'He's smart,' says Shiv, pointedly.

They lean in to take a look.

Kai whistles. 'Six! Nice!'

Jay is nodding. He looks impressed too.

'Did you have face down, hood up—or no camera?' asks Shiv.

An icy wave runs down my spine. I didn't think about that.

'Face down,' I lie. A white lie, because an old man with a bell on his shop door is unlikely to have CCTV.

'Good news,' says Shiv, 'because once the police have your mugshot it's a nightmare. Gets passed round everywhere, for ever. Some shops print them out and stick them next to the till, just in case you come in. We need to sort you out with a bike, don't we?'

It feels like the bike is no longer my problem. It's our problem. And I'm guessing 'sort out' doesn't mean 'buy one'.

'Yeah. What about the train station?' says Kai. 'Plenty of choice on Friday. Start of the holidays, everyone's out late for a party then takes a taxi home. They don't want to cycle, so they leave their bikes till morning. Big mistake.' He grins.

'No one home at mine tomorrow. We can make some plans.' Frazz doesn't say much, but when he speaks, everyone listens.

'Cool,' says Shiv. 'Bring your black book, Jack. We can show the others your pieces.'

'I wanna get started,' says Kai, rubbing his hands together. 'Take the paints down to the old shack and dress it up.'

We all nod.

'Yeah,' murmurs Jay.

The little voice deep inside and far away whispers *stop stop*, but it's getting fainter. Soon I won't be able to hear it at all.

Crew 2

'Jack, stay behind, please.'

Students pour through the doorway like sand through a timer.

'Jack.'

I put my bag on my shoulder and pretend not to hear.

Heads turn.

'Mr Willis wants you,' mutters the sand to my right.

I hang back until everyone has gone, then turn to face Mr Willis.

He's waiting behind his desk, arms folded. He isn't smiling or frowning. He has the same neutral expression Mum wears when she's planning to talk things through.

'Pull up a chair.'

We both sit down. Mr Willis rests his elbows on the desk.

It's more serious than I thought.

'Jack, your teachers have mentioned that you're not turning up for lessons. I checked with the nurse, and he says you haven't been to sick bay this week.' He hesitates. 'Do you want to tell me what's going on?'

I am silent.

He rests his chin on his thumbs. After a minute or so, he says, 'I had hoped we could talk about it.' His tone has changed. It's quieter, melancholy even. I know this tone. It's the *I'm sorry about your dad* tone.

I am silent.

The far-away voice is trying to tell me something, but I can't make out the words.

I'm glad Mr Willis made me stay behind. I hadn't realized, but the chance to be silent is what I wanted. The chance to be blank. To show that despite what everyone expects, I don't feel anything right now.

I am aware of something else happening, something which I don't like. Beneath the nothingness, a kind of pressure is building. A dark, swirling mass. I'm not sure where it's come from or what's feeding it. If I open my mouth, I sense that the darkness might be tempted to escape, and I'm not sure I'll be able to stop it.

'Jack, I'm here every morning, lunchtime and after school. I'm always ready to listen, when you're ready to talk. If you'd rather chat to a different teacher, that's fine too.'

The swirling mass is gathering momentum. I need to get up. I need to leave.

'Don't miss any more lessons, Jack.' Serious voice has returned. 'You're a good student. Next term is key for decisions you will be making later in Year Nine. You need to keep your grades up.'

A tightness is spreading across my forehead. I reach for my bag.

'Right. See you tomorrow morning.'

He chooses to ignore the fact I am already half-way to the door.

I'm late for Spanish. I walk quickly, but my feet don't stop when I reach the languages wing. They speed up. I walk past the room where Dan and Johannes will have started their lesson. The seat next to Dan, empty again. I keep moving until I reach the gym. I pause outside the changing room doors. There are voices, laughing and talking. A class getting ready for PE. I can't stay in the corridor. I think about waiting in the toilet. But my body has a life of its own. I elbow my way in, through a jumble of T-shirts, arms and feet.

'Wrong class!' someone shouts. A few heads turn and there is laughter.

'Message for Mr Sim,' I say, pushing past.

Mr Sim is by the door, holding a stack of multi-coloured cones.

'Left my bag by the fence,' I say. 'I'll be quick.'

Mr Sim nods. 'Hurry up.' He doesn't question why I've walked through the gym to reach the playing field. He doesn't seem remotely interested in what I'm doing, as long as I leave the changing room. Which is good, because anything more than a glance would have revealed that my bag is on my shoulder, tucked behind my right arm.

I walk briskly across the field, and duck under the hole in the fence.

I tap my phone to refresh the screen. Frazz lives at the far side of the high street. I don't know the area well, so I follow the map to a terrace of pebbledash houses with tarmac drives. A sticker on his letterbox says No Cold Calling. I can't see a bell, so I lift the flap and let it drop with a thud. Through the frosted glass, a figure grows larger. For a second, I wonder if this is the right house, then the door swings open.

'Jacky-boy!' says Kai. 'Don't wait there like an advert for school-skiving, get inside.'

The sitting room is stuffy. Music is playing from something out of sight. Shiv and Jay are sitting on a shiny black sofa, Frazz is slumped in a huge beanbag by the window. I wonder how long they've been here.

'Show us your book, show us your book,' encourages Frazz, before I sit down.

'Picassooo!' hollers Jay, pattering a drum roll on his legs. I can't tell if he's mocking me. I assume he must be, as he hasn't seen anything I've drawn before.

The zip on my bag sticks. I give an extra tug, then slip the A4 sketchpad from the inside pocket, passing it to Frazz. He turns the first page, and the second without comment. As he turns the third, he begins to shake his head.

'Whoah,' he mutters. 'You did this?'

'Hand it over!' says Jay, leaning forwards.

Frazz snatches the book away. 'Patience, my friend.' He carries on flicking slowly through.

'That's based on Zephyr's old-school style.' I point. The book is upside down for me, but I know every sketch.

'Is he from round here?' asks Kai.

'He's from New York. One of the best. That's ROA.'

Frazz is shaking his head again.

'What did I tell you?' says Shiv.

'These two are like Basquiat's early stuff.'

Frazz frowns. 'Nope.'

'French. You should check out his work.'

When he's finished, Frazz passes the book to Jay, then Kai.

It's getting dark when Frazz looks at his phone.

'OK, you have to leave. Seriously. My dad will be back in ten minutes, and he will be super annoyed if his house is full.'

Everyone gets to their feet. Kai opens the window.

I stuff the sketchpad back in my bag.

'Those are some stellar pieces you have in that book,' says Kai, 'but get a move on.' He waves me to the door. 'You do not want to annoy Frazz's dad. Ever.'

Fire

I smooth down a page in my sketchbook. I've added nothing for three months. My pencil hovers above the white space as I picture the outline for a new design. The shapes I want to make. No letters or animals. I want to create something abstract—swirling and wild and dark.

Downstairs, the front door clicks shut.

Silence.

Then Mum calls, 'Hello, darling, are you OK?'

I stare at the blank page. The shapes evaporate, until I am left with just a pencil and some paper.

The stairs creak a dull tune, then my door swings open.

'I wasn't sure you were here!' Mum's tone is cheerful, but criticism lingers in the spaces between the words. When she's here, I should drop everything and make the most of it.

I'm lying on my bed, so she perches on the chair by my desk. She's wearing smart clothes which look out of place. Dad used to sit in that chair. He'd spin it round then sit astride, resting his arms on the back like he was riding a horse. He was always smiling. That's how I remember it. Although for a split second, I find it hard to see Dad's face. His features won't settle.

'Are you sure you're OK, darling?' Mum leans forwards, searching my face for clues.

'I'm fine,' I mutter through clenched teeth.

'Jack, I've had another call from school.' She hesitates. 'They told me that you've been absent from a number of lessons. They would like me to go in for a chat. With you. They want to see us together.' She pauses again, taking a deep breath, before adding, 'We can fix this, Jack.'

There is no heaviness this time. Instead, the dark swirling thing from earlier swoops in. The word 'fix' is for furniture and plates. For cuts and grazes. What's happened to me cannot be fixed. No one can 'fix' a hole that wasn't there before. There are no edges to sew up, no sides to glue. I sense the whirlwind spinning out of control.

Mum is staring at me, her eyes wide. The rest of her seems frozen, unmoving.

There's nowhere for me to go. Nowhere to hide. I can't run to my room. She's already here. I can't run to the kitchen. She'll just follow. I toss the sketchbook aside and lurch towards the door. I need to get out before the whirlwind bursts free.

'Jack!' Mum calls as I thud down the stairs. 'Jack, I want to help. Just talk to me. Don't shut me out.'

I try to block her words. Instead, they echo round my head as if trapped in a jar *talk-to-me-don't-shut-me-out*.

I'm not shutting her out. She was never in.

I rush through the hall, running my arm along the shelf, sweeping a jumble of pots and figures to smash or fracture on the wooden floor.

'Jack!' Mum is shouting now, from the top of the stairs.

I pull on my trainers and run outside, slamming the door behind me. Cold air bites at my face. I keep running. I don't have a plan. My feet take me in the direction of the park, so that's where I'll go. The gate will be padlocked, but that's not a problem. The whirlwind carries me over the metal fence and onto the frosty grass. I keep going, past the playground. Past the football pitches. I know where this path leads, where my feet are taking me. The low brick building comes into sight. Dark holes gape where the windows should be. On the left, three squares reflect night-white clouds, signalling their presence. Inviting me. They know why I'm here. I scout around the walls, looking for chunks of brick or concrete. With four lumps cradled in my arms, I retreat ten metres, then raise my hand and throw. The first brick crumps against the wall with a powdery thud. The second explodes amidst a spray of glass. Another flies from my fingertips so fast that the window smashes, followed by a thud as my lump of concrete strikes a wall within the building. As the third window erupts, I hear shouting.

'I see you!' a voice cries.

I start running, my feet following the route Shiv and Jay took on their bikes. Towards the gap in the hedge, leading to a quiet road.

My breath comes in short gasps as my legs and arms pump up and down. It feels good, but I can't maintain this pace.

Something is moving across the grass much faster than the man, something which grabs at my sleeve. I stumble to the ground, rolling, chin tucked to my chest. A dog with short, dark fur clamps its teeth around the edge of my sweater, growling with a menacing rumble. I jerk my arm away but the dog tugs it down. Its head is level with mine.

Footsteps thud nearby.

'Let go!' I hiss, pulling my arm again.

'I wouldn't do that,' snarls a man, panting to catch his breath. 'He might take a real bite.'

I don't want the man to see my face, but the dog won't let go. If the man calls him off, and I sprint away, the dog will be faster. I'm trapped. I keep my head down anyway. There's someone with the man. Two pairs of feet wait a few metres to my left.

'You've got two choices.' The man's voice has a hard edge, but now it sounds more matter of fact. 'I can take you to the police station, and you can explain to them what you were doing. That's choice number one. Choice number two is that I take you home, and you can tell your parents what you were doing.'

My mind races. I don't want to go home. Ever. I don't want to apologize in front of Mum. The police station would be better. Anything would be better. But something makes me hesitate. The voice is shouting from far away. I can't hear it, but somehow I know what it's saying. Dad wouldn't like me to go to the police station. But Dad's not here.

'He won't answer. Let's just take him to the station.' I glance up. The voice belongs to a tall boy with a thin face. He's older than me. Maybe eighteen or nineteen.

'Who are you with?' asks the man.

'No one,' I say. 'On my own.'

'Throwing rocks at a building. That's a fun thing to do on your own,' says the boy.

'Leave him. He can explain to the police. Let's go.' The man starts walking.

The dog growls as I get to my feet.

'Drop it! Drop!' the man commands. The dog releases my sweater and trots alongside, its hot breath near my hand.

Beyond the hedge is more fence and a gate. It's shut, but not padlocked, and swings open with a screech.

'Wait,' I say. The man spins round. 'Take me home.'

'Right.' His voice is business-like. 'You go in front. Casper will keep you company.'

'Hope it's not far,' grumbles the boy from somewhere behind me.

I guess Casper is the dog.

Again, I have a weird sensation that I'm watching myself, that these events are happening to a different me. But different me lives at the same address, with the same front door.

Ash

I open my eyes and stare at the ceiling. There is movement on the landing. Padding footsteps. The handle of my bedroom door creaks gently down. Something hovers in the doorway.

'Jack,' a voice says softly. 'It's time to go to school.' The voices pauses. 'It's late. I can drive you in, if you want.' A hand slides quietly down the doorframe. 'It's the last day of term. I thought you might like to see your friends.' There is no mention of important choices, big decisions. The future.

I roll onto my side and pull the covers above my head.

The handle creaks gently up. Footsteps pad downstairs, but the front door doesn't open. Or close. Mum hasn't gone to work.

Heaviness seeps through my bones, pinning me to the bed. Today is the last day of term. Beyond that, the holidays. Two weeks of festive family time. Two weeks of togetherness.

I replay last night's events in my head. The look of surprise on Mum's face when she opened the front door to find me arranged like a carol singer between the man and his son. Casper growling by my feet. How she smiled as the man spoke, trying to intuit the situation. How her smile faded, and she began nodding, apologizing, telling two complete strangers about Dad.

Once they had gone, she followed me into the kitchen. I sat down, waiting for the chat, wanting it to be over with as soon as possible.

She filled the kettle with water. Wiped down the surfaces. Almost as if I wasn't there. I thought perhaps she had forgotten about me. Absorbed in thoughts about school, vandalism, her pointless son. Then she pulled up a chair. We sat in silence for a while. That's how the worst chats begin. The ones that go on for ever, concluded only when issues have been defined, addressed, discussed, boiled alive.

The silence continued. I began to wonder if this was a new type of 'chat', one where I was simply given space to think about what I'd done in a meaningful way.

I turned to look at Mum.

She looked back, and whispered, 'I miss him too, Jack.' A tear splashed on the table. She brushed it away, like the toast crumbs at breakfast time. Then she pushed back her chair and returned to the kettle.

Pancakes

My phone won't stop buzzing.

I drank the water which Mum left next to my bed. I ate the toast.

She rolled up my blind to let the light in but didn't mention school again.

Now the square of light is fading. Dusk is falling.

I haven't moved all day.

I reach for my phone.

There are too many updates, too many messages. I scroll through, not reading, until I spot one from Dan.

Still up for my house tomorrow? Ben wants to know if you're throwing up again. D

I keep scrolling, past the messages from Shiv and Ben, then place the phone on my bed.

After a few minutes, I pick it up, and scroll back to the messages from Shiv.

No show today?
Midnight at car park. Don't be late. Time to choose your present!!

I won't be late. I won't be there. I wonder if they'll steal me a bike anyway. Choose my 'present' for me.

Mum is on red alert. There's no way I can slip out.

Or bring back a bike.

Or get up.

The heaviness which has pinned me to the bed, has smothered the fiery whirlwind too. The only thing which seems to drive it away. I wonder what will happen now.

'Jack.'

I open my eyes.

For a second, I struggle to work out what time it is. Which day it is.

Sunlight creeps around the edges of my blind. Daylight. That means I've been asleep for twelve hours. It's Saturday. The first day of the holidays.

I become aware of someone close by. I turn my head. Mum is silhouetted in the doorway. Always in the doorway.

'I've made pancakes,' she says softly. 'Please come and eat some with me.'

She disappears, back downstairs. A smell of burnt bread drifts into the room.

My stomach growls.

I stretch my arms out in front of me, to check they still work, then push myself out of bed. My body feels strangely weak. I suppose I've barely eaten anything for the last few days.

I follow the smell, down to the kitchen table, at the centre of which rests a plate, piled with enormous pancakes. The pancakes have pale edges, and blackish centres. A new smell mingles with the aroma of burnt bread. Mum is by the hob, prodding bacon in a pan.

'I've heard that in Canada, people like to eat pancakes with bacon and maple syrup. I thought I'd try it. We don't have maple syrup but I think honey will do.'

She piles the bacon on a plate, placing it in front of me. Then she takes a pancake for herself, folds a rasher of bacon within and squeezes honey on top. She takes a bite and frowns but carries on chewing.

My mouth is dry. I reach out and take a pancake. I try one without the honey. It tastes pretty good, so I start a second. The twisting grumbling sensation in my stomach fades, the weakness too. Instead, the listless feeling whisps around my chair, waiting to pull me upstairs to bed.

Mum takes another pancake, then seems to forget about it. She puts the lid on the honey jar and has a sip of tea.

'I've been thinking. In fact, I was up most of last night, thinking,' she says, almost to herself. 'Perhaps we both need to get away from here for a bit. Go somewhere else. For a break,' she adds quickly, almost nervously.

I stop eating and look at her.

She fiddles with her knife and fork, straightening them on either side of her plate, even though they are already straight.

'It's—well, I'm not sure either of us wants to be here—at home—for the holidays. The accommodation would be free. A work contact has offered me—us— somewhere. It was supposed to be in January, but I can bring it forwards. We just need to pay for flights.'

I try to process what she is saying. A holiday. Me and Mum, alone together. No friends. None of my stuff. Potentially endless chats. My mouth feels dry again. I finish chewing, then push my plate away. I sense Mum following my every move.

I want to go back upstairs. I can pull the covers over my head. I don't need to travel far away, only to feel trapped there instead. Two weeks will pass, and the holidays will end. After that, it will be school again. Choices, futures, taking things seriously.

My only escape is Shiv—which reminds me. I need to reply. Explain what happened yesterday. That I was under house arrest. The whirlwind stirs in my chest.

Other thoughts drift in, uninvited—the voice in my head when I was walking towards the police station; a tear splashing on the kitchen table.

Mum is silent. It confuses me. She normally expects a speedy response. Pushes for an answer.

I want her to push now. To force me to choose. To rouse the whirlwind, so that it can sweep me away in its swirling rage.

What will I do for the next two weeks? Before I can block it out, an image of Christmas Day flashes through my head. Two places laid for lunch. An empty chair by the sitting room window.

I shake my head.

'Darling?' I hear the concern in her voice. She takes another sip of tea, which must be cold. Then carefully, quietly, begins to pile things onto her plate, to take over to the sink.

'When?'

She pauses, a hand frozen around the honey jar.

I repeat, 'When? When would we go?'

'Is tomorrow too soon?' She doesn't smile, but there is a brightness to her eyes, which wasn't there seconds before.

Pack

I brace my arms above my head as an avalanche of laundered shorts and T-shirts tumbles from the shelf, thumping to the floor in half-folded heaps. I doubt they fit, but there's no time to try them on or buy new stuff. Mum said pack clothes for all seasons—except winter, the only season for which I actually have clothes.

A blue suitcase lies open on my bed. It smells of my last school trip. A pen lid pokes out from one corner of the lining, glued in place by a fluffy, wrapper-less sweet.

I pile everything inside, squashing it down to make space. I need to cram in as much as possible. Apparently, *we won't be doing any washing while we're away*. A few pencils, scattered on the floor near my desk, have disappeared. Perhaps bundled up with my shorts. I can't be bothered to fish them out. I pause for a second, then reach for my sketchpad, tucking it beneath some T-shirts. Inside my rucksack, I stuff a tablet, chargers, earpods and a book.

As I close the wardrobe door, something clanks against the bottom edge. A can of aerosol paint rolls softly onto the carpet, followed by another. Most of the clothes which held them in place are now in my suitcase. I think for a moment. One by one, I remove the other four and slide them all under my bed. I'm not sure why. No one's going to set foot in here for two weeks.

I check my clock. The taxi will arrive in thirty minutes. Mum has been packing and planning since breakfast time. Calling airlines and contacts. Emptying out the fridge. Washing the bins. It's like we're going away for months, rather than weeks. She hasn't hassled me once. Not even when she realized there was an hour to go, and I hadn't started packing.

I thud the suitcase downstairs, one step at a time, leaning it next to Mum's large silvery-grey hard-shelled version. Her hand luggage is a rucksack made from thick fabric in the same shade of silvery-grey. I don't remember ever seeing them before, which seems weird as she travels all the time. I guess I just didn't pay attention.

She emerges from her office with a pile of notebooks and papers. She seems surprised to see me waiting in the hall, and wraps her arms more tightly around the pile, before turning back to her office.

I head upstairs to see if I've forgotten anything important. Anything I might miss. I open the drawer beneath my bedside lamp. Inside, sits a small stack of books and on top of them, a photograph. The photo is creased, white lines criss-crossing the edges, but the image is clear. A man and a woman smile into the sun, hair whipping round their faces. In front of them, a little boy holds out his hand. In his palm nestle three or four white shells. I can almost feel the warmth of the sun, the breeze on my face. There aren't many pictures of me, Mum and Dad together. This is my favourite because it was Dad's favourite. He kept it inside his wallet.

There is a loud knock on the front door. I slip the photo into my back pocket and turn out the light.

The taxi is early but I don't mind. I'm ready.

Spark 2

We speed along the motorway. The taxi has an unfamiliar smell, like peppermint mixed with perfume. Every few seconds, headlights flare in the dark, highlighting Mum's face. She's been staring out of the window for most of the journey, frowning slightly as if trying to solve a problem. No doubt I am the problem.

Normally when we go away, I want to know everything—where we will stay and what we might do. I like to daydream about it. This time, I don't feel curious. I prefer not knowing what will happen next. My head feels strangely blank. I don't even know which airport we're flying from.

My phone buzzes.

Are you OK?

It's Dan. I didn't show up yesterday. I didn't message him either.

Going away for a bit. On the way to the airport with Mum. Be in touch when I'm back.

He sends a thumbs up.

It's like having another mum.

Perhaps I should let Shiv know I'm going away too. I didn't show up on Friday, and I didn't message him either.

I choose a shorter version. I don't think he'll be interested in who I'm going to the airport with. He's never met my mum.

Going away for a bit. Be in touch when I'm back.

I check my phone a few times, but I suppose not everyone replies instantly like Dan.

The taxi slows and we enter a maze of junctions and enormous blue signs directing us to various terminals and car parks. Mum tears herself away from the window and begins searching through her bag. When the driver makes a joke about handbags, she gives a tight smile. Normally she loves talking to people. One of my mum's special skills is getting along with anyone she meets—in the supermarket, on a walk. Dad used to call her the environmental-and-friendly anthropologist.

On holidays, especially, Mum was a magnet for cheerful conversations about the weather and good places to eat. I guess this holiday is different.

We glide along polished white floors, pulling our cases towards Departures.

I've never heard of the place we're going to, but that doesn't matter. I don't recognize half the destinations listed on the screens.

Mum announces that dinner on aeroplanes takes for ever to arrive and we need something to keep us going. I'm not really hungry, but I don't have the energy to say no. Anyway, what would we do instead? As we sit down to eat, my phone buzzes. A message from Shiv.

Have you quit this crew?

I feel hot. I want to stand up, walk around, but there are people everywhere. What does Shiv mean by *have you quit*?

No. Def not.

I type, while Mum orders.
My phone buzzes again.

No show Fri? No paints? No respect?

My head whirs.

Back in 2 wks and will make up for it. There was a problem.

I say nothing that will lead to questions about home. They always end up in the same place. Shiv doesn't reply.

As Mum walks towards the table, another message appears.

2 wks.

That's all he says. I wait to see if there's more but there isn't. I don't know how to fix things, but in two weeks' time, that's what I'll have to do. The hot feeling has passed, but my palms feel clammy.

'OK?' asks Mum, sliding back into her chair. 'Don't worry, the food's on its way,' she adds, mistaking whatever expression I'm making for one of hunger.

I nibble at some chips. There are chicken nuggets and a small pot of grapes too. Mum's food choices seem to have been inspired by a toddler's birthday party. She doesn't appear to be hungry either, which is weird, since *something to keep us going* was her idea.

When half the nuggets and most of the chips have gone, she checks her watch then leans away from the table, searching left and right for an information screen.

'We have to go!' she says. 'The gate is closing.'

She mostly tapped the table and fiddled with her napkin while we were eating. I wonder why she didn't check earlier to see whether the plane was boarding.

'This way,' she calls, dodging round a couple walking arm in arm. No one pays us any attention. I guess people running to catch their flights isn't that unusual.

As we reach the gate, half the passengers have boarded. We show our passports, then join the back of the queue.

Mum is still catching her breath, when she says quietly, 'There's something I need to tell you.'

I glance at her face. She isn't smiling. 'Jack, this isn't exactly a holiday.'

'What do you mean?' I ask, unsure that I've heard correctly. Beeping scanners make it harder to pick out the words.

'When I said we should go somewhere else for a break, I meant a break from home.' She rummages in her bag for the boarding passes. 'The reason a work contact offered me—offered us—free accommodation is because, rather than a holiday, this trip is, well... This trip is also kind of related to the project I was helping with.'

I swallow. Trying to untangle her words. Mum is usually so precise.

'Are you saying that this is, in fact, a work trip?' We've nearly reached the flight attendant checking passes.

'I mentioned an indigenous group—at risk.' She's in control again. 'And funding to support conservation efforts in the region.' I vaguely remember her saying something. She holds out the boarding passes. 'Everything is in place, and I was due to go in January, but I wasn't sure that would be wise.'

We shuffle along a tunnel connecting the aeroplane to the terminal building. Her voice is low but seems loud in the enclosed space. No one else is talking.

'I had spoken to Dan's parents about whether you might be able to stay with them, but we felt perhaps now wasn't the right time.'

The spark flares in my chest. 'You mean, you planned to go away with work and leave me with Dan's family, but after careful consideration, you all decided that wouldn't be quite *right*?' The whirlwind rushes in, spinning wildly. She didn't want to go away with me at all. It wasn't because we both *needed* to. She just had nowhere else to put me. They don't have kennels for children.

'It didn't seem like a sensible time for me to be away.'

'You couldn't wait to get away but decided against it. Not because of what may be right for me. Because you just can't trust me. That's all, isn't it?' My voice is getting louder. A woman turns round. The others in the queue stare ahead, towards the entrance to the plane.

'No—that's not what I'm saying at all.' Mum's face is pale.

'Why,' I say through gritted teeth, 'did no one think it might be sensible to speak to ME? To ask me what I THOUGHT!?' I am shouting.

There are murmurs. One of the flight attendants moves away from the plane entrance, towards us.

'Please step over here for a moment,' he says, smiling warmly, but with his arms raised as if catching a massive beach ball. 'Is everything OK?' he asks, still smiling. He is talking to both of us, but looking at me.

I hear myself mutter, 'Everything's fine.'

He nods, but doesn't move, or lower his arms.

'If you need a minute before boarding, that's not a problem.'

Now that I'm safely corralled, the other passengers turn to stare.

'I'm fine,' I repeat.

After a few seconds, he steps aside, and we board as if nothing happened.

I guess for him, nothing really did.

Burn 2

I am next to the aisle, half aware of passengers squashing luggage into overhead lockers, bumping my leg as they squeeze past, searching for friends, ignoring cabin staff. Half aware of the engines' roar, the pressure of my headrest as we lurch upwards, burning gallons of fuel to propel 400 tons of metal into the sky.

The rest of me is focused on calming the storm inside my head, dark and swirling, blowing reason aside. I want to shout, to bang my fists on the armrests, to set the storm free.

Words spiral within, tossed about in the maelstrom. Fragments of conversation. *Get away, go somewhere else, have a break*—that's what we *needed*. Mum lied to me. Tricked me. She saw that I was confused. Tired.

I will never forgive her.

Sometime later, the lights in the cabin dim. The storm still whirls, but more slowly. I'm running low on power. It's late. How late, I have no idea. My phone is switched off and the aeroplane screens display a different time zone.

'How long is the flight?' I don't turn my head, but sense that Mum is awake.

'Twenty hours. We fly for twelve, then land to refuel. The second flight is four hours.' It's almost as if she has been waiting for this precise question since take-off, her answer prepared for an instant response.

'When do we fly back?' I need to know exactly how long we will be stuck on this 'trip' together.

'I am hoping two weeks.'

I snap my head round to look at her. 'Hoping?' Despite what she's done, she sounds chatty. Relaxed.

Two weeks is all I have. *2 wks.*

Shiv and the others are waiting for me. Waiting for the paints. They want me around. They're annoyed when I'm not. That's why Shiv's message was unfriendly. They need me; me and my black book. But if I'm gone too long, they might decide Jay was right and that four is better than five after all. At Frazz's house, Shiv mentioned moving in with his cousin. A small place where no one could tell them what to do. He'd be his own boss. Maybe there would be space for me. Shiv didn't say how they would pay for it. We'd figure something out. One thing's for sure: I can't stay at home.

'There are some time factors I can't control, but I'm aiming to move things along as quickly as I can.'

Mum speaks slowly, choosing her words with care. She's worried about the whirlwind. About me making another scene.

'Sounds like the perfect holiday,' I mutter.

'No, not perfect,' she replies. 'But—' She stops herself from saying more.

'But what?' I ask, my voice growing louder. 'But at least there will be a swimming pool, wi-fi and surfing in the sea?'

A girl peers down the aisle at me. I stare back until she disappears behind the headrest.

'I was going to say, it doesn't have to be awful either.'

I wait for the swirling anger to flare, sweeping away my thoughts, flinging me from this seat, but nothing happens. It simmers but doesn't spark. Perhaps I'm too tired.

I try to picture the accommodation provided by a 'work contact'. A flat somewhere, in a town or city. I guess there must be an office nearby where Mum will be working. That means I'll have the days to myself. I can look round. On my own. Last year that would have seemed weird. Frightening, maybe. But now, I like the idea of wandering around, looking for street art. Of Mum not knowing where I am.

My eyes feel heavy. I begin to drift in and out of sleep without properly resting. There is a bump which jerks me from side to side. People start to clap. Clicks fill the plane as everyone unclips seatbelts, stretches, stands. The first flight is over. I glide through the polished aisles of a different airport, and board another plane—or the same one, refuelled. I have no idea. The cabin lights turn on and off. Meals arrive at random times. Finally, I fall into a deeper sleep, until gradually, I become aware of something tapping my arm.

'Jack, Jack, we're coming into land,' Mum says.

I blink. My eyes are dry and the daylight seems brighter than usual. Seconds later, the cabin lurches as we touch down. People start to clap again, a few even cheer.

Feeling dazed, I gather my things and stuff them into the rucksack. Everyone else appears alert and ready to go.

The old lady in the seat next to Mum asks her something in a language which sounds both harsh, and slightly musical at the same time. I recognize it. Mum often speaks it when she's having work calls, or when she's having a cup of tea with my avó—my Granny.

'*Sim, estou de férias com meu filho.*'

The lady looks over and smiles. Whatever she's saying is obviously about me.

We glide more slowly through this airport even though it's a fraction of the size. We queue to show passports, wait for luggage.

I don't ask, but it seems Mum has been here before. She knows her way without checking the signs. I follow in her wake like a little kid.

As we approach the exit, she drags her case to one side and beckons me to follow.

'I need to make a call.'

She speaks quickly, laughing and gesturing with her free hand. I wish I knew what she was saying. I notice that the phone she's using is different to the one she has at home.

It's almost as if work Mum and home Mum are two separate people with two separate phones and two separate lives.

There was only one version of Dad. The one who

stayed at home. With me. I feel an ache somewhere deep inside. How would he feel about me coming here, far away, with the version of Mum that has better things to do?

'It's OK, they're outside,' Mum says, as if I have some idea of who 'they' are.

Before I can ask, she's hurrying towards the doors, the silver suitcase clicking along behind like a shiny hard-shelled version of me.

We step into a pocket of hot air. I take a few steps forwards, wondering whether I'm in the path of an air-conditioning outlet, or the exhaust of an engine.

My face begins to flush. I pull my hoodie over my head, then rummage in my rucksack for a bottle of water, desperately trying to cool down.

'It gets everyone like that when they first arrive!' calls a nearby voice. It's sing-song, and I can tell the owner of the voice is smiling.

I spin round, confused. A woman with shiny dark hair is walking quickly towards us.

'*Bem-vinda de volta! É tão bom ver você. Fiquei muito triste com suas notícias. Sinto muito!*' The woman wraps her arms around Mum, then turns to me, smiling. '*Você trouxe seu filho. Ele é alto!*' She raises her hand in the air, as if trying to guess how tall I am. It's definitely not a competition she is going to win. The top of her head is level with Mum's shoulder.

'Jack, this is Maria.'

'Sorry, sorry,' says Maria. 'I sometimes forget which language I'm speaking! It's so great to meet you, Jack. I've heard a lot about you.' Maria's eyes sparkle as she talks.

'Come, you must be tired. The car is this way.' She walks briskly in the direction from which she appeared. Turning now and then to flash encouraging smiles as the gap between us widens.

My legs seem fixed in idling mode. Or a different time zone.

Mum slows down to join me. 'I always stay with Maria,' she says, as if that explains why I'm on a work trip, on a different continent, in a city I've never heard of. 'She's like family.'

My stomach performs a strange kind of flip.

Family.

Maria

Maria is waiting beside an enormous 4x4 with wide wheels. Next to it crouches a small silver car dimpled with dents. On the rear window is a sticker of a parrot. She unlocks the boot to the silver car. It's barely wide enough to fit one suitcase, yet she somehow squashes both in. Squashes mine—since Mum's is solid.

'Jack—Jackinho!' Maria's eyes sparkle in the rear-view mirror. 'I'm so happy that you're here. There is *so* much to show you. *So* much to see.'

She revs the engine too hard, then crunches the gear stick into reverse position. We lurch backwards.

'How much language do you understand? *Nada mesmo? Um pouco?*'

I hesitate. 'A little.' There's no point lying. Mum knows I understand some of what Maria is saying. I've listened to her speaking to Granny often enough.

'*Maravilhoso!*'

Maria makes me feel as if it's not just speaking her language that's brilliant—I am somehow brilliant too.

She starts chatting to Mum in the passenger seat.

I'm glad to be left alone. My T-shirt is sticking to my back, and my leg is sticking to the rucksacks piled on the seat next to me. I lower the window and lean into the warm breeze, watching the buildings change from pale office blocks to square white houses. As we leave the main road, the smart white houses become smaller, made from large pinkish bricks which look rough and unfinished. My forehead bumps against the window as we bounce over potholes and swerve round dogs, asleep on the tarmac.

The car slows, stopping outside a rectangular house with a sloping tin roof, sandwiched between two smaller red-brick buildings. Not exactly the metropolis. Thunder rumbles overhead.

'My house!' says Maria, as the first fat raindrops begin to fall. Seconds later, it sounds like a giant is drumming their fingers on the car roof. 'Jack, you bring the rucksacks. Me and your mum will carry the cases,' she yells.

I cross the few metres separating car and house, dashing through the doorway after them. My hair and shoulders are soaked, but my face has cooled down, and the air feels less sticky.

'OK, we're here!' says Maria. 'I suggest dry clothes, then we eat, then perhaps you need to sleep?' She looks first at Mum, then at me. 'Are you tired, Jackinho?' She asks the question as if the whole city has paused, awaiting my answer.

'I didn't sleep much last night,' I mumble.

'*Bom*. Then I will show you your room.'

We climb narrow stairs to a tiny landing area. The house seems very compact. I'm surprised I have my own room. Maria opens a door to our right.

'Here you are.' She gestures with her arm, as if revealing first prize. 'Only unpack what you need for tonight. We'll see you for some *comida* in a minute.'

I wheel my case towards the single bed and sit down. I need to keep moving, or else I might fall asleep right here, in my wet T-shirt.

As I change into dry clothes, I glance around the room. The walls are covered with paintings. Some no bigger than my hand, others as wide as my suitcase. They are mostly of wildlife, butterflies and birds, but some are more abstract. There is a slim wardrobe and a small desk. On the desk are photographs in

92

silver frames, pens and pencils, and a tray filled with small brightly coloured bottles of nail varnish. For the first time, I notice there is a scent. Like bananas mixed with chocolate, or coffee. I wonder if this is the spare room which Mum usually stays in when she visits. I think back to Maria, showing me in with a flourish—first prize. Perhaps second prize is sleeping on the sofa?

A new smell creeps beneath the door—a rich, spicy aroma. My stomach twists uncomfortably. I step onto the landing, closing the door behind me. For a moment I am disoriented. There is another door to my right, and to my left, some kind of sitting area, but the lights are switched off. The smell must be coming from downstairs.

I follow the sound of voices to a table laid with small bowls. Steam rises from a pan in the centre, behind which sits Mum, like a genie who forgot their outfit.

'We're having *tacaca*,' she says, her eyes shining a bit like Maria's. 'It's my favourite dish. Also, Maria is a very good cook.'

'Oh, stop!' says Maria, carrying another bowl filled with something beige and floury. 'I'll get a big head!'

I know that Dad's favourite dish was spaghetti Bolognese. I had no idea Mum's was *tacaca*.

She ladles thick yellow stew into my bowl. Giant prawns bob to the surface, along with a greenish vegetable.

'You're supposed to drink it from the bowl, but I don't mind if you prefer to use a spoon,' says Maria, holding out the plate of floury stuff. 'This is *farofa*. It's good for soaking up *tacaca*.'

I eat a spoonful of stew. It's sour, and a little bit sweet. I'm not sure I like it. As I take another spoonful, my mouth heats up. I try to cool the spiciness with a piece of the greenish vegetable, and the heat develops into a tingle. My mouth is going numb. I'm having some kind of allergic reaction. The numbness spreads along my tongue. I place the spoon on the table a little too hard, just as Maria makes a strange squeaking noise. Her hand is clamped over her mouth and I wonder if she's having the same reaction, then I notice her shoulders trembling—she is laughing.

'*Desculpe, desculpe!* I'm so sorry, Jack, I should have warned you.' She shakes her head. 'Jambu leaf is a natural anaesthetic. When you chew it, your mouth will tingle a little bit. We eat it all the time. I forget about the tingle.'

I glance at Mum. She smiles back. She's eaten jambu leaf before. She could have warned me, instead of joining in with the fun—at my expense.

'Eat *farofa*, that will help,' she says.

The numbness is fading, but I eat some *farofa*, then another spoonful of *tacaca*, being careful not to scoop up anything green.

'You must taste this too.' Maria lifts a plate of fried fish. When I hesitate, she adds, 'Don't worry! It won't make you tingle, or turn you blue, or anything unexpected.' Her smile lifts every part of her face.

'Thank you for dropping everything,' Mum says, between mouthfuls. 'I didn't give you much warning.'

'Well, I'd already started planning, so it's just a little earlier, and earlier is better.'

Mum and Maria chat quietly. The *tacaca* has left a warm sensation in my mouth, which I don't mind. Waves of exhaustion lap slowly over my body and I'm about to head upstairs to bed, when the front door slams.

'*Olá, querida!*' Maria calls.

I spin round. A girl, about my age, slings a bag on the floor then walks past the stairs towards the table. Mum pushes back her chair and throws her arms wide.

'*Que bom te ver!*' she says, as they hug. The girl leans over and kisses Maria on the cheek. They have the same straight black hair.

'Jack, this is my daughter, Pakoyai. Pakoyai, this is Jack.'

I nod my head, 'Hi.'

'Nice to meet you,' says Pakoyai, in a tone which suggests it's not nice at all. She flicks her hair away from her face, and the scent of bananas and chocolate drifts over.

I try to recall where I've smelt it before. As Pakoyai pulls up a chair and ladles *tacaca* into a bowl, I remember. My room. No wonder she wasn't pleased to see me. My room isn't the spare room at all. It's Pakoyai's room.

Confession

For a moment I have no idea where I am. I rub my eyes and stare at the pictures on the wall, at the desk. Then it comes back to me. The *holiday*. The little house in the middle of nowhere. Mum's other *family*. I pick up my phone to check the time, but the battery's flat. I wonder which day it is. Maybe Tuesday? I need to keep track of how many days have passed.

If it's Tuesday, then I'm guessing Mum will be working today. Perhaps I can ask Maria which bits of the city are worth exploring. Clearly not this part. I reckon Maria would be totally cool about me looking around on my own. Perhaps she can persuade Mum. I suppose I'll need money too.

I wonder what Dad would think of this place. We would talk about the *tacaca*, about the heat. Dad's opinion would help me to make sense of it all. At home, I could always imagine what he might say. Here, he seems just out of reach. Silent. I remember a few days ago, when I couldn't picture his face clearly. Maybe while I'm here, it will fade faster. I get out of bed and slip the photo from the pocket of my jeans. Dad smiles up at me. Unchanged.

As I get dressed, there are voices in the small sitting area. I push open the bedroom door. Mum and Maria are kneeling on the floor, surrounded by piles of clothes or kit of some kind. They look up.

'Sleep well?' asks Mum. 'It's nearly midday.'

'What should I feed you—breakfast or lunch? Or both?!' Maria seems delighted by this conundrum.

'I don't mind,' I say, 'as long as there's no jambu.' She smiles. 'I thought you'd be going into the office today,' I say to Mum. 'Or are you going in later?'

Maria looks from me to Mum. 'What office, *amiga*?' she asks, frowning.

'She said this was a work trip, so...' I pause, watching Maria's eyes growing wider.

'Oh *céus*, Sofia—you didn't tell him?'

Mum shakes her head, slowly.

'OK. I'm going to get some food ready.' Maria picks her way between the small heaps on the floor, leaving me and Mum alone.

'Tell me what?' I ask. 'I thought discovering that our holiday was actually your work trip was the main surprise.'

Mum closes her eyes for a few seconds.

'I mean, what other surprises can there be? Did the office burn down or something?'

Mum shakes her head again.

I stare at her, my brain whirring. 'What's going on?'

In her calm, steady, *we need to talk* voice, Mum says, 'Most of my work involves travelling around. But not to offices. Very early tomorrow morning, a jeep will arrive.'

'Why not use a car like everyone else?'

'Because it's taking me to the rainforest.'

The swirling darkness begins to stir. 'Well, that's perfect. You've brought me halfway round the world, so that you can leave me with people I barely know. Although I guess it doesn't feel like that, since they're *family* to you—the one you actually spend time with. I should have just stayed at home.' Mum is staring at me, frozen between piles of clothes. 'Is this your new way of doing things? Just make sure we're on the same continent, then it's business as usual?'

As soon as the words have left my mouth, I wish I could suck them back in. The darkness hurled them out, now they fizz and burn in the air between us.

A pan clanks somewhere downstairs.

'No.' Mum's voice is so quiet I can barely hear it.

'No? Then how is it different?'

'You're coming with me.'

Fire 2

I hear them shouting.

'Stop! You'll get lost!'

But I want to get lost. My feet thud along the tarmac, crunching through a layer of grit.

The roads are straight lines, like rungs on a ladder. There are no curves, no bends. When the street ends, I turn right.

My thigh muscles burn, but I keep going. Thunder rumbles in the purple-grey sky.

I turn right again, keeping to the middle of the road. A dog barks, straining on its lead as I pass. There are no pavements, but also no cars.

Another roll of thunder booms overhead. Fat raindrops fall, puffing up dust. I pause, turning my face to the sky. Water splashes on my cheeks, running down my neck. Salty sweat stings my eyes. Within a few seconds, my T-shirt is soaked.

I keep moving, more slowly. Tea-coloured puddles form in the road.

I think about Mum. About her impulse to get away. About how it seemed to make sense. Now I see that it wasn't an impulse at all. It was a calculation. The only way she could go without leaving me at home alone. I'm like an extra piece of luggage. Excess baggage.

I break into a run, splashing through puddles, ignoring the squelch of my socks.

No one wants me here. I expect Maria would like me to go, after hearing me shout at Mum. At least with Pakoyai I know where I stand. I stole her room. She can't wait for me to leave. No one is waiting for me at home, except Shiv, and I might have messed that up too by being here.

Running feels good. The only thing which stops me from shouting, from smashing things up. The further I go, the freer I become. Right now, no one knows where I am. I don't know where I am. I realize that I don't even know Maria's surname, or the name of her street. No one I meet will know me. For the first time in three months, I am just a boy with brown hair. Not the boy whose dad died. I slow down again.

My legs are shaky. I've had nothing to eat since the night before. I wonder where I can get some food. I don't have any money. I haven't seen any shops.

There are voices, and a boy steps from beneath the covered porch of a house, heading my way. As he approaches, he says something. When I don't answer, he stops, blocking my path. He speaks again with a less friendly tone. He's younger than me, but doesn't step aside, so I push him. I push him hard. He stumbles onto the muddy road. My arms moved before I could think. Now there's a buzzing in my head, urging me to offer my hand, to help him up. But my arms hang limply by my sides. The boy looks at me, eyes wide. I stare back, and the buzzing grows louder as I realize that he is scared.

Two more boys emerge from the house. They are older, maybe eighteen or nineteen. They walk quickly, speaking angrily, pointing to the boy on the ground. One of them goes to help him, the other steps towards me. He shoves me, his hands thumping against my rib cage. I stumble, but stay on my feet. He shoves me again, more forcefully. I fall backwards, stones cutting into my palms. He kicks at my right leg, catching me in the thigh. The muscle feels cold with pain. He aims another kick, then pauses.

'*Deixe-o em paz!*'

There is a shout. A girl holding a blue umbrella makes shooing motions with her free hand. The older boys jeer, but as she gets closer, they move slowly on. I feel my cheeks burn.

When the girl is a few metres away, I recognize her. It's Pakoyai.

'Jack?' She frowns at me through the rain. 'Did those *bandidos* attack you?'

'Not really.'

'What are you doing here?'

'I—' There's no good way of explaining why I'm sitting in a puddle. 'I went for some fresh air.'

'Do you know how to get home?'

'No, but—'

She clicks her fingers and starts walking. 'Well, lucky that I've finished my shift at the cafe. I'm heading there now.'

My feet take a few running steps to catch up. Feet which, seconds before, were running in the opposite direction. My right leg buckles as pain burns across my thigh. I limp, trying to match her pace. I have to tell Pakoyai I'm not coming back to the tiny house filled with people who wish I was somewhere else. She seems so sure I will follow. She'll want to know where I'm going instead. I can't say that I don't know. She'll laugh.

Even though she's just saved me from being beaten up, I glare at her.

Pakoyai flicks her dark hair over her shoulder. She's looking straight ahead at the fading figures of the three boys. She doesn't offer to share the umbrella, but I'm soaked anyway. She doesn't seem interested in talking either. Talking might take my mind off the throbbing pain.

'So you were at work?' I ask.

'Yes.'

'But—shouldn't you be at school?'

'Well, you're not. We have holidays in this country too. I was helping my uncle out.'

Her English is perfect.

'It's his cafe?'

'Yes, it's his cafe.'

Her tone suggests I've just put two and two together, with the help of a calculator.

I notice that my heels are rubbing against my wet socks. My jeans also rub, pulling on my hips as if twice their normal weight.

'Does it ever stop raining here?' I don't know where my questions keep coming from.

'Sometimes. It's dry in August. But this city is in the middle of the rainforest, so I guess there's a clue.'

Pakoyai clearly doesn't want to chat. Perhaps it's time to stop trying.

I look around at the houses instead. Anything to distract me from the pain. They're squashed close together, assembled in a hurry—at least that's how it seems. Lumps of dried mortar cling to the edges and several window frames are missing. Porch tiles creep onto the road, making the whole street feel like a slowly growing cement-brick monster.

Pakoyai side-steps an extra-large puddle, then takes something from her pocket. My stomach flips when I realize that we're outside her house. I wasn't expecting to be back so soon. If at all. I haven't thought about what to say, or how to deflect a 'chat'. I glare at Pakoyai again, but her face is still obscured by a curtain of black hair. I bet she can't wait to tell everyone she found me in a puddle. That she rescued me.

The door swings open and a spicy, savoury smell wafts out. No one rushes to meet us or demands to know where we've been.

'Oi, *xodó!*' Maria calls from the kitchen.

She sees me and throws her arms in the air. 'Jackinho! Well done, you've brought Pakoyai!'

'Actually, I brought him,' mutters Pakoyai in English, so I know it's for my benefit.

'You're soaked!' says Maria, placing bowls of food on the table. 'Leave your wet things by the door. I can dry them for you.'

She doesn't seem to have noticed that I'm also covered in mud.

'T-shirt and trousers! Everything wet. Then come and eat.'

It feels as if nothing has happened. As if shouting at Mum and running out of the house occurred in a different street, with a different boy. There is no special 'tone', no meaningful pause, allowing me to explain myself.

A puddle has formed on the tiles beneath my shoes. I kick them off, piling my muddy jeans and T-shirt on top, then run upstairs. My cheeks burn, even though Maria and Pakoyai are in the kitchen with their backs to me.

'Oh!' Mum looks up from the sofa. The mounds of kit have disappeared. Instead, several bulging rucksacks and holdalls are stacked by her feet.

'I'm glad you came back to eat with us.' She smiles, although unlike Maria, I can tell from Mum's voice that she is upset.

'I got wet,' I say, to explain why I'm only wearing pants.

She nods. 'Better put on something dry.'

She doesn't mention the blueish-red bruise, blooming across my right thigh.

I unzip my suitcase. Half of my clothes seem to have gone. As I rummage for a T-shirt and shorts, raised voices float up through the ceiling. Maybe Pakoyai is telling Maria about what happened. Or perhaps she's just demanding to know how long I'm staying. Or why I came in the first place. That makes two of us. She'll be delighted when Maria tells her that I'll be leaving first thing.

I have no money to fly back on my own. So rainforest it is. If tomorrow is Wednesday, that means ten days until we head home and I can start to sort my life out—the way I want it to be. I'll fix things with Shiv and when he finds a place with his cousin, I'll join them. Then Mum can travel as much as she likes. She won't need to pretend she wants me around any more. I won't get in her way, and she won't get in my way. I'll have *my* new family.

Then it dawns on me where my clothes must be. Mum has packed them in one of the rucksacks. Even my clothes must dance to her tune.

Jeep

There is a gentle tapping noise.

'Jack, it's time to go. The jeep's here.' Mum's voice drifts through the door.

I rub my eyes. No light filters between the curtains. It's still dark outside.

I dress and pad downstairs. My trainers are lined up neatly by the mat. Someone has cleaned them. I slip one foot inside. The trainer is completely dry. I wonder how. I haven't spotted any radiators.

'Oven baked, low temperature.' Maria appears by the front door, clutching some paper parcels. I must look confused, because she adds, 'Your shoes—I oven baked your shoes, not breakfast!' She raises the armful of parcels. 'Sleep well?'

I nod. 'I guess we'll see you when we're back.'

Maria shakes her head. 'Jackinho, always making me smile.' She pushes her feet into a pair of plimsols. 'We're all going!'

I turn to see Pakoyai drifting downstairs. Unlike Maria, she isn't smiling.

'How do you think your mother will find her way in the rainforest without me?' Maria adds.

Rather than tell Maria I have no idea what we'll be doing in the rainforest, or why we're going, I just nod again, and slip on my other trainer.

Outside the air is warm. There's a strange scent, like the smell of soil, or wet leaves. For the first time since we arrived, I can imagine a forest beyond the city, its tendrils winding along the streets as we sleep. Despite the temperature, I shiver. I wonder where we'll stay when we get there. I hope, wherever it is, the walls are thick.

The jeep's engine growls into life. Mum and Maria climb into the front seats. Pakoyai opens the rear door and shuffles as far as she can towards the opposite side. When I slam the door it makes a metallic *clunk*. There's nothing fancy about the jeep. It's a tin can on wheels. I look for a button to lower the window, but instead find a handle to turn. I literally have to wind down the window.

A deep voice says, 'There are no cushions and

flashing lights, but this will take you anywhere, and bring you back again. If it's Bluetooth that you want, then maybe stay here.'

A pair of brown eyes glare at me from the rear-view mirror. They sparkle like Maria's, but not with fun.

'Lucas! I'm sorry, Jack, you have to forgive my brother, he was working last night. He's not had much sleep.'

'I'm fine,' he replies, in a voice which echoes the growl of the jeep. The engine revs and we creep forwards. The street is deserted, except for a few dogs blinking in the headlights.

Pakoyai taps at her phone. I slide mine from my pocket. No one's expecting to hear from me any time soon, but I check my messages anyway, at least I try to—there's no signal. I open a few apps but nothing works.

'UK phone?' Pakoyai turns her head. I nod, surprised that she's taking an interest. 'Won't work here,' she says, rolling her sweater into a pillow.

I put my phone away and glare at the road, ready to lash out at Pakoyai or Lucas, or whoever speaks to me next. But that's what Pakoyai wants—for me to lose my temper. She's taunting me. Perhaps Maria told her that I ran off yesterday. That I lost control, and that's why I was out in the rain. I try to ignore the gentle tap of her fingers on the screen, and the dull ache in my leg.

Dawn melts the glow of the headlights. Buildings emerge from silhouette to reveal people shaking out rugs or heading off to work. The single-storey houses change to flats and office blocks as we approach the city centre, towards hustle and people, away from muddy streets and dogs.

A large grey building looms to my left, a huge shape sprawled along one side. I press my cheek against the window frame for a better look. As we draw level, the shape morphs into the face of a man, painted in black and white. The man is staring into the clouds, his features so realistic he resembles a black and white photo. Kaleidoscope lines of colour radiate from behind the face. It's bright and serious and completely brilliant. I spin round as we pass, trying to fix the image in my brain. It's the best street art I've ever seen. I wonder how long it took, how the artist made the lines so straight, the face so real yet so huge. It must be fifteen metres high. Did they have permission to paint it? Questions buzz around my head, blowing the angry sparks away. I want to stand in front of the face and stare up, feeling the power and the size of it for myself.

I want to know if there are more, to wander round the city and find them.

Instead, I'm in a rusty jeep, with no wi-fi or phone connection, heading to the jungle.

Ten days, I remind myself. Ten days.

Mud

Our jeep rattles towards the edge of town, where the road rises to bridge a wide, dark space. I rub sleep from my eyes as the dark space shimmers and twinkles. Seconds later, buildings melt away as we cross—not a space, but an immense river. The opposite bank is shrouded in mist, drifting up from the murk.

'It's black because of rotting leaves and plants from the rainforest,' says Pakoyai in the same matter-of-fact voice she used to tell me my phone wouldn't work.

I carry on staring through the window, saying nothing. Pakoyai seems to know what I'm thinking, which is annoying.

Mum and Maria had been chatting quietly with Lucas. As the river rushes beneath, their voices grow louder and the conversation seems livelier.

Maria turns round. 'Both OK?' She smiles, passing something to Pakoyai—one of the paper parcels she was clutching earlier. She holds another out to me, then hesitates. I realize she is staring at my hand.

'What did you do?' She frowns.

My palm is peppered with cuts and scratches.

'I fell over,' I say, waiting for Pakoyai to contradict me, but she doesn't.

'I have antiseptic in the first aid box. We should treat those when we stop, in case they become infected. The rainforest isn't kind to cuts and scratches. But right now—we've left the city, Jackinho! That means it's time for breakfast! We'll be driving for a while, so no need to eat in a hurry.'

'Unless this rust-bucket breaks down, then you'll have to get out and push.' Lucas's brown eyes are fixed on me again. His gaze is intense, like before, but his voice is softer.

They seem glad to leave the city. I wonder whether Pakoyai is too. I don't have her mind-reading skills.

I peel back the paper. Nestled within the parcel is a large chunk of French bread filled with cheese and an orange-coloured fruit resembling mango. I take a small bite. It has a strange earthy taste, like chestnuts, and a slight sweetness which is delicious with cheese.

'Do you like the *tucuma*, Jack?' Maria asks.

'Mmm,' I mumble.

'Good! Because we eat *a lot* of *tucuma*.'

As I chew the first bite of my enormous sandwich, we reach the far end of the bridge. Beyond the mist, there are no apartments or office blocks. Palm trees and bushes creep up to meet the tarmac. Trunks and branches lean in every direction. It's as if we've passed through some kind of magic gateway. There are no hard edges, there is no order. We are completely surrounded by green.

A phone rings, snatching me from the fairy-tale weirdness.

'*Pronto!*'

Maria speaks quickly into her phone. Pakoyai stops tapping on hers and looks up. Maria shakes her head, then says something quietly to Mum.

The mood in the car has changed again. There is no more chatter, just the rustle of paper as we eat.

I don't want to talk, so I guess it doesn't matter.

My eyes begin to close as the warm air and jet lag take effect. When I open them again, I'm not sure how much time has passed. It must be several hours, but seems like several days, because the view from my window is unlike anything I've ever seen.

Tarmacked road has melted into orange mud. On either side, trees tower twenty metres high, exploding into sprawling canopies of green. Closer to the ground is foliage so dense I can't see beyond it.

The jeep glides slowly through the mud, only gaining traction at the drier edges. We tilt left then right, as if we're skiing. A growling lump of metal seems totally out of place here, but it's a growling lump of metal I do not plan to leave, at least until there's more tarmac to step onto.

I want to know how much further there is to drive, but everyone is sleeping except for Lucas. The muscles on his arms bulge as he grips the steering wheel, trying to prevent us from skidding. His eyes flick up to the rear-view mirror, then back to the road—if you can call it that.

The air is hotter and stickier than in the city. My T-shirt has pasted itself to my chest. Even my knees feel damp. I want to have a shower. I also wonder whether there will be air conditioning where we're heading. Pakoyai, her face still resting on her jumper, hasn't broken a sweat.

My stomach growls. If it's nearly lunchtime, that means another half-day has passed.

Only nine and a half to go.

Bruno

'*Pare!*'

The jeep skids to a halt. I lurch forwards and my shoulder thumps against the door handle. I sit back in my seat, rubbing my shoulder and scanning the road ahead to work out what's happening. A boy appears by Lucas's window, grinning.

Maria leans across, one hand on her chest. '*Tome cuidado!*' she calls. The boy nods. I recognize the words. Maria is telling him to be careful.

He's small, maybe four or five years old, and I wonder what he's doing here on his own. What he's doing here at all.

'Oi, Bruno!' Lucas thrusts his arm out of the window to shake his hand.

How does Lucas know him? A boy in the middle of the road, miles from anywhere.

This journey can't get any weirder.

Bruno runs round to Maria's door and she lifts him onto her lap. Once he's settled, Lucas drives slowly on.

Somehow, I didn't notice that the trees and bushes have begun to retreat. We are approaching a small clearing. Nine or ten huts with palm-leaf roofs cluster at its centre. They appear to be levitating but as we draw closer, I spot wooden stilts, raising them several metres above the ground. Next to the huts, lapping around the bottom of tall, reedy grass, is a river. This river isn't black. It's tea coloured like the puddles in the city streets. It's as wide as several houses and flows with a surging force that suggests it could happily sweep you away unless you were a very good swimmer, or a fish.

The little boy, Bruno, is sitting on Mum's lap now, chatting as if her knows her. Perhaps he does. A few days ago, I would have felt surprised. Now he just seems like another piece in the jigsaw of her other life. The one which doesn't feature me or Dad.

Lucas parks the jeep by the nearest hut. Bruno rushes off, emerging seconds later with a man who I guess might be his dad. Lucas greets the man, throwing his arms around him with a warmth that seems at odds with the way he speaks. Pakoyai yawns and stretches, then pulls on her trainers.

Surely we can't be stopping here for long? Maybe we need to refuel, or to collect something. I have no idea what.

As Pakoyai tugs at one of the rucksacks on the back seat and eases it onto her shoulders, the terrible truth begins to dawn. We have reached our destination. This is where we're staying.

How can it be necessary for Mum to come here for work? What can she do in this place that couldn't be figured out via phone or email? I don't want to ask. I can't make myself sound friendly, or even pleasant right now, and I've had enough of Lucas glaring at me. Also, I can imagine Mum leaping on any sign of interest as an indication that I might have started to forgive her for dragging me out here and lying to me.

I step into the orange mud. Bruno looks over. Perhaps he hadn't realized there was a fifth person in the jeep. He runs towards me, and I hear myself saying, '*Meu nome é Jack.*'

'*E o meu nome é Bruno,*' he grins.

In the distance, thunder rumbles.

'Jack, come and say hello.' Mum beckons.

Bruno takes my hand, steering me towards the others, grouped near the hut.

'*Eu me chamo Paulo.*' Bruno's dad smiles warmly. He says something about being pleased to meet me. Perhaps news of my disappointing behaviour hasn't spread this far yet.

Fat raindrops patter on the mud.

'We should get everything in before it starts for real,' says Maria.

The clouds here seem to sense when we're about to unpack a vehicle.

'Don't worry,' says Pakoyai, passing me on her way to the jeep. 'We're only here for one night. Tomorrow we'll be staying somewhere *really* special.'

Blue

'Keep still.' Maria tips a few more drops of bright yellow liquid onto a piece of cotton wool and dabs the cuts on my hands. It stings, but I try not to wince. 'Why didn't you say something before?' She tuts, but it's not an annoyed tut.

Rain drips from the roof, carving an outline of the house within the mud.

'May I see?' Mum leans over, but I close my hands.

'They're fine,' I reply.

Maria tuts again, reaching into the medical bag for something else.

'I need to take your temperature. Open your mouth, please.'

'But I feel OK,' I say, confused. 'It's just a few scratches.'

'It's not for you.' Pakoyai's voice drifts over from a stool near the window—a small square cut from the woven palm leaves. 'It's for the people you meet. In case you're harbouring something horrible. We all need to do it,' she adds, perhaps to deflect from the rest of her comment—the nasty bit.

'In case we've brought city germs to the rainforest,' explains Maria. 'We always check.'

I open my mouth, then snap it shut, almost biting the thermometer in two as a creature the size of a small cat darts towards Bruno.

'*Ei!*' Maria yells.

I leap up, clutching the thermometer. Bruno looks at me in surprise, completely unfazed by the animal which has draped itself around his neck, unfurling a long fluffy tail. Gently, he coaxes it onto his lap, holding it out for me to take. The creature dangles from Bruno's hand, peering at me through enormous round eyes, then yawns, revealing rows of sharp little teeth.

'*Ela se chama Lala,*' he says.

'Er, *olá, Lala*. Maybe later—*talvez mais tarde,*' I say.
Bruno looks disappointed.

'It's a night monkey,' says Pakoyai. 'Orphaned. Bruno rescued it. He doesn't usually let other people hold it.'

I sense everyone's eyes on me as I walk back to Maria. There is an unpleasant prickling sensation across my neck. I try to remember when I felt like this before. As I reach the chair, I remember. I was in the art shop with my bag full of paint, walking down the aisle towards Dan.

Paulo appears in the doorway and says something about food.

'Lunch is ready!' Mum announces.

Everyone murmurs *obrigado* and heads towards a ladder, tied to the doorframe with twine. It must be seven or eight hours since we had our jeep-breakfast. I don't even mind getting soaked again, if it means we can eat.

We gather beneath a large gazebo with a palm-leaf roof, next to a long table with benches either side. On the table rests a huge fish, steaming gently within an even larger leaf. There are wooden bowls containing chopped banana and *farofa*. Lala grabs a chunk of banana and scampers to the end of the table with it.

Paulo serves Lucas first. He perches on the bench as he eats, pausing occasionally to join in with the conversation. Everyone still seems in a serious mood, speaking fast and softly, so I can't figure out what's going on. Halfway through the meal, Lucas gets to his feet.

'Where's he going?' I ask no one in particular. This isn't good. Lucas and the jeep are our connection to the real world. To the city. My only means of escape.

'He has to get back tonight. He can't leave the cafe any longer,' says Mum.

I'm about to ask how soon he'll return, when I feel a heavy hand on my shoulder.

'Jack,' Lucas says in his gravelly voice, 'be careful, OK?'

I want to shrug my shoulder away, annoyed that someone I barely know is giving me lessons in common sense, but when I look him in the eye, I see that Lucas isn't patronizing me. He is worried.

Blue 2

I hardly sleep, even though when I went to bed, I was almost too tired to take my shoes off. *Went to bed* is an exaggeration. We are sleeping in fabric hammocks suspended from the roof, which began to creak when Paulo slung mine from the same beam as the other four.

Unperturbed by our first encounter, or perhaps because of it, Bruno's monkey takes a special interest in me. As soon as Bruno is asleep, she walks back and forth along the edge of my hammock, eventually settling on my legs. I should have realized that night monkeys don't sleep much after dark.

Mum gave me a mosquito net to hang from cords snaking down from the ceiling. I think it was designed to fit around a bed. With no frame to secure it at the bottom, it droops towards me like a weird, annoying shower curtain. Mosquitoes still buzz in my ear. If they buzz near the monkey's head, it leaps up to catch them, using my legs as a springboard.

Pakoyai said that tomorrow night we would be staying somewhere really special. The more exhausted I become, the more vividly I imagine a large wood cabin with soft beds and a gentle breeze from the air conditioning. Although deep down, I sense that's not what she meant by *special*. Then my thoughts drift to Lucas and his bizarre warning.

Their family seems expert in cryptic messages.

Thoughts about Dad drift into my head too. I try to push them away. So far from the city and anything we did together, the horrible silence is growing. I reassure myself that back home, everything I see, everything I do, brings his voice to life.

It's weird, because I thought that's what I wanted to leave behind.

I wonder what Dan would think if he could see me now, dangling beneath a roof, somewhere in the rainforest. Dan likes camping. He likes hiking and knows obscure facts about snakes. He once told me that there's only one poisonous snake in the whole world. When I said that was rubbish, he said that poisonous animals unload their toxins when you eat them, like the garter snake, which is small and harmless—unless you eat one. Most snakes transfer toxins by biting, so they are venomous, not poisonous. Dan would be having a great time right now. As long as he had some rules to follow.

When I try to imagine what Shiv would think, I can't picture him here without Frazz, Jay and Kai. I'm not even sure what Shiv likes, really, but I'm pretty certain he would hate being away from the city. That would suit me fine. Once we have a place to share, I don't plan to leave the city either. There wouldn't be any creatures making weird noises, like the low croaking sound I've been listening to since dusk. Or the squawks and howls from further away. I'm glad we're protected by the walls of the hut. Even if they are made from palm leaves.

Light filters through the window holes. The roof creaks as people stir. I glance over to Mum. She seems to find sleeping in a hammock no different from sleeping in a bed at home. I half expect her to climb out wearing work clothes and clutching her satchel, before heading down the ladder. At least it's too humid to leave Post-it notes with dinner instructions.

'Did you sleep OK, Jackinho? Check your trainers for spiders,' Maria calls, her head disappearing through the doorway.

'Come and get something to eat.' Mum approaches the edge of my mosquito net. 'I'm afraid we need to be on the move again soon.'

Her eyes have the same sparky energy as at the airport.

I wonder what surprise she's going to share this time. I'm not sure I have the stamina to care.

I'd give anything to step into a cold shower. Instead, wearing yesterday's clothes, I make my way towards the shelter, from where a plume of smoke spirals upwards, carrying the smell of toasting or frying.

As I sit down to eat, Bruno brings his bowl across and perches next to me. The monkey comes too.

'*Lala, não!*' Bruno laughs, when she tries to steal my bread, settling instead for a line of ants crawling along the bench towards me. She picks them off one by one, examining them closely before popping them in her mouth.

Maria and the others are deep in conversation once more. They appear to be asking Bruno's parents a lot of questions. Pakoyai seems much older as she nods and gestures alongside Maria. I expect she thinks I fit in perfectly at the five-year-old end of the table.

They clearly don't plan to involve me in their discussion, so when I've finished eating, I lie in my hammock and wait. I hadn't considered who might drive us to where we'll be staying tonight. Or in what. I haven't seen any vehicles. It occurs to me that I haven't seen another road, apart from the one we arrived on.

I begin to doze when footsteps tap on the ladder. The hut explodes with activity, as Pakoyai starts untying the hammocks and Maria begins piling rucksacks in the centre of the room. Bruno zigzags between them, chasing Lala.

I rub my eyes and get sleepily to my feet. I guess it's time to leave.

'Feeling tired?'

I didn't spot Mum approaching.

'I'm fine,' I say, unsticking my T-shirt from my back.

'We're going to load up the boat.'

So that's why there's no road. We're travelling down the rapids instead. Of course.

'Jack, I know you don't want to talk to me.' Mum's eyes flick around my face. 'But there are a few things you need to know before we set off.'

She is speaking softly, but I get the feeling it's to keep me calm, not because what she's saying is for my ears only.

'You don't need to know what I'm doing here if you don't want to, but things have changed a little since we set off. We're going deeper into the rainforest.'

'I thought that was part of the plan anyway—*your* plan?'

She closes her eyes for a second. Behind her, the hut is emptying as bags and rucksacks are passed through the narrow doorway.

'Yes. But it's going to be much... riskier than we thought.' She nods to where Maria is standing. 'Jack, it might be dangerous.'

The word feels strangely flat.

There is no hint of a smile on Mum's face. She brushes a few damp strands of hair from her face but her eyes remain fixed on mine.

'I've been talking to Bruno's parents and they said that it would be OK if you stayed here. They said that Bruno would like it,' she adds quickly, because my face can't hide the whirlwind stirring inside. Mum is doing what she does best. Leaving me somewhere, so that she can do what she wants.

I feel my breath quicken.

'So you're leaving Pakoyai here too?' I say, through clenched teeth. Lala bounces across the room to watch.

'Pakoyai is coming. It was just a thought,' Mum adds. 'It's up to you. It's your choice.'

Only none of this is my choice. I don't want to be here at all. But if Pakoyai is going, I'm not staying here to be babysat. There's no way I'll give Mum the easy option of leaving her burdensome son for someone else to look after.

But the main reason I want to go, is one she won't suspect at all.

Danger.

River

The boat is long and thin, like a banana cut in half. It sits low in the water and it wouldn't take much for one side to tip beneath the tea-coloured river water, sinking us in seconds. Paulo does his best to distribute the bags evenly, then beckons me over. He points to a spot between two rucksacks.

'Step into the centre,' advises Maria.

'So that you don't tip it over,' adds Pakoyai helpfully.

The jetty is made from the same pale wood as the boat and slopes to one side, so I lose my balance before I've even left the shore. Paulo reaches out a hand to steady me. The others clamber in without assistance, but then I guess they've all done this before.

We perch one behind the other. Pakoyai at the bow, then me, Mum, Maria and Paulo at the back, his hand resting on a tiny outboard engine which must propel five people and all the bags. Bruno waves from the huts, Lala perched on his head like a hat, as the engine growls into life, emitting a ball of smoke. It whines and revs as we leave the jetty, gliding so slowly through the surging water that I wonder whether we might stop entirely.

'We're travelling upstream,' says Mum, 'against the flow of the river.' In case I don't know what upstream means. 'It will be slow-going. On the way back we may not need the engine at all.'

We rock from side to side as Paulo navigates a sharp bend, then steers towards the bank where the water is calmer, but low branches dangle at head-crunching height.

Half an hour of frenetic packing and loading has worn everyone out. For a while, no one speaks. Not even Maria.

Mum's words circle in my head as the engine sputters in the background. *It might be dangerous.* She hoped that would put me off. But I want something to happen. I want something to make me feel scared or excited. I'm tired of feeling angry. Only angry.

It's early in the morning but the air is warm. Heat radiates from the milky water, cancelling out any breeze created as we move.

I dangle my hand in the cool river water.

'*Nãu*!' There is a shout from the back of the boat. I snatch my hand back. '*Não faça isso*,' Paulo repeats less urgently.

Pakoyai spins round.

'Did you put your hand in the water?' she asks. When I don't answer, she says, 'That's a good idea if you don't need all your fingers, or maybe your arm.' I raise my eyebrows but stop short of rolling my eyes. 'There are piranhas in there which would love a snack. Or if you want to take us all down, you could always get the attention of a black caiman.'

'OK, I get the message, David Attenborough,' I snap.

'Jack, that's enough!' Mum says.

I rub my hand across my forehead. Pakoyai has a gift for making me sound ridiculous.

A voice whispers deep inside my head. The voice I thought had gone. It's quiet but persistent. *You made yourself sound ridiculous*, it chides.

Eight days until we fly home, I think. Eight days. Then I can silence the voice for ever.

'Jack, we should put antiseptic on your hand. The one which went in the water,' Maria calls.

Mum rummages in one of the bags and pulls out a small green box. She finds the bottle of yellow liquid before handing the kit to me.

'The floor's wet. Put this on your lap while I fix your hand.'

'I can do it myself.' I reach over to snatch the bottle and my elbow knocks the first aid kit from my lap. It disappears beneath the water with barely a splash.

Mum and Maria gasp.

I close my eyes. I know this is bad.

Mum turns to Maria. 'Was that everything?'

Maria nods. 'Antibiotics, antihistamine, anti-inflammatory, bandages...' She bites her lip. 'We can't replace them. We'd have to get Lucas to bring supplies from the city. They wouldn't arrive for at least two days.'

'That would be too late.'

'Too late,' Maria nods. 'We should abandon the trip. It's pure recklessness to go without medical supplies.'

Pakoyai turns round. 'What happened?'

No one answers.

'I knocked the medical kit overboard,' I mutter.

Pakoyai tilts her head to one side and smiles a fake sort of smile. 'What really happened?'

Her fake smile begins to fade, and I realize that even Pakoyai didn't think I could be *that* stupid.

My chest tightens. If we'd gone on a real holiday, none of this would be happening. I could dangle my hand in a river without something biting it off. We could buy first aid supplies in a supermarket. Not that we'd need them—on a real holiday.

'I think we should keep going. It might be our only chance,' Mum says.

At first, Maria doesn't answer. Then I hear her say quietly, 'We take no unnecessary risks.' She pauses. 'Perhaps we should ask Paulo to wait for us too.'

'With the boat?' Mum replies. 'We planned for six days, with supplies for eight. But that was based on feeding four people, not five. Anyway, his family needs him,' Mum adds.

'OK,' says Maria. 'Let's ask if he can return after four days. We're just going to have to walk fast.' She turns to Paulo.

'*Sim, sim. Sem problemas,*' I hear him say.

No problem. Although problems are the only thing we seem to have plenty of.

Disconnect

The sky is turning purplish grey. Thunder rumbles above the trees. It feels as if we are drifting slowly through another world. A world where guidebooks and planning don't count for much. There are no car doors slamming. No radios or sirens or alarms. It makes me feel as if I'm drifting too. I have a sudden urge to open a fridge door or turn a tap on. To do something which connects me to a place where people are in charge. Not plants.

A strange chirruping fills the air, getting steadily louder. Like thousands of insects warning us to turn back, to go away. It's bizarre that so much noise can be made by something too small to see—at least from the boat.

Sitting in a line makes it hard to talk. Not that I want to, but I might feel less like I'm slipping away from reality. From Dad. Pakoyai spends her time watching birds flying low across the water, catching insects, only turning her head when there is a loud squawk or cry.

After an hour or so, the river narrows, its edges blurring as vegetation creeps in from the shore. Trees balance on stilt-like roots, suspended high above the water. Decaying logs drift in clusters and grasses sprout amongst the gentle ripples. Paulo lowers the revs, allowing us to manoeuvre around the obstacles, or nudge them gently aside.

A few minutes later, Mum taps me on the shoulder.

'Paulo says we'll be at the set-down point in twenty minutes. Can you let Pakoyai know?'

'I heard,' Pakoyai says. 'Twenty minutes.'

'We'll eat when we stop,' Mum adds. 'It's easier than passing food along the boat.'

Better than me dropping it overboard, is what she means, but doesn't say.

When she mentioned lunch, my stomach began to growl. I'm also desperate to stand up. My legs are twitchy after four hours of sitting. Flies and mosquitoes buzz constantly around my head, and even though I'm covered in insect repellent, red patches bloom on my hands where some have taken a bite.

I have no idea how Paulo knows which way to go. I can't see any route through the swamp. I'm also wondering how we get from the boat to the shore. I've seen nothing resembling solid ground.

'Have you ever left the city before?'

Pakoyai's voice takes me by surprise. She has twisted round on her seat to face me.

'Er, sure, lots of times.'

I wonder why she suddenly needs to know.

'Have you ever been to the rainforest?'

The answer to that question must be obvious, but she's staring at me, waiting for a reply.

'Nope.'

She nods slowly, as if mulling something over.

'Then I have one piece of advice,' she tilts her head, 'it might save your life.'

I wait for the life-saving tip, my interest piqued.

'Don't touch.'

'Don't touch what?' I ask.

'Don't touch anything.'

'Brilliant. Thank you,' I reply. 'I feel ready now.'

Pakoyai raises her eyebrows.

'She's right,' Maria says softly from the back of the boat. 'It's a good way to avoid anything which stings or bites.'

'Or is poisonous,' says Pakoyai.

I want to snap at her. To say something annoying back. Something equal to *don't touch*, which is great advice—if you're five years old. But an echo of the little voice reminds me that this would be a good way to make myself look ridiculous again. I'm trapped. In this conversation, in this boat, in this rainforest.

I decide instead to focus on an earlier conversation. The one where Mum and Maria discussed cutting the trip short by a few days. Perhaps we'll be home before *2 wks* is even up. For some reason, this doesn't make me feel better.

The croaking-chirping-squawking noise has grown so loud, that at first I don't realize the engine has stopped. Pakoyai reaches for a short wooden paddle by her feet.

'*Vire à esquerda,*' Paulo calls.

She dips her paddle in the water to the right of the bow, so that we turn gently to the left. I duck as we pass beneath the sprawling branches of a huge tree, balanced on spider's-leg roots.

The water is calm here, and we are moving so slowly, that I notice ripples and splashes nearby. Something breaks the surface a few metres away, near a swarm of small black flies. I can't tell whether it's a fish or a frog. It seems weird that creatures leap from the water to catch things in the air, but

I guess it's no stranger than dangling a hook in the water to catch a fish.

'There might be electric eels around here,' says Mum. 'They can hit you with 500 volts.'

I spin around to face her. There is no hint of a smile on her lips. She's not joking.

But it's OK, because I've had my rainforest survival course.

No harm will come to me because I won't be *touching* anything.

Green

'Jump!'

I push away from the edge of the boat, landing on spongy grass. My arms windmill as I tip back towards the eel-infested river.

'Grab the root!'

I snatch at a branch-like root beyond the grass. My fingers close around its soft bark, allowing me to pull myself further up the bank, away from the water and the eels.

'Well done, Jackinho!' Maria calls. 'There is nothing worse than wet feet in the rainforest, especially when you're going to hike.'

I thought that there was nothing worse than touching things in a rainforest. My feet are dry, but I did grab a tree root, so perhaps I'm about to be stung or poisoned anyway.

143

Pakoyai has vanished within the foliage, having leapt so nimbly from the boat that she made it look easy.

'Take this.' Mum holds out a rucksack. 'Don't lay it flat on the ground. Ants will crawl straight in.'

Even a tiny amount of activity makes me sweat. The humid air clings to everything. I wipe my forehead with a damp sleeve. At least we're in the shade now.

I follow the route Pakoyai took, brushing past giant palm fronds. She's in a small clearing, using a broken branch to sweep aside the dead leaves and sticks. It's going to take a while to clear the whole forest. She pauses to unzip a side pocket of her backpack.

'Hold this, please.'

I'm beginning to feel like a porter. She passes me some paper bags and a bottle of water just as the others appear, carrying what's left of the luggage.

Maria arranges the rucksacks in the swept area, propped against each other in a lumpy pyramid. She unfolds one of the paper bags and lays it on top, making a table for lunch. We eat standing up. I guess because it reduces contact with deadly things.

'Jack,' Mum says in her serious tone, 'this is a remote section of the rainforest.' Not exactly a surprise. She places her half-eaten sandwich on the square of paper, giving me the full *expert-anthropologist-professor* stare. 'The families who live here aren't settled in a village but prefer to move around where the hunting is best, or the fruit is ripest.' Why is she telling me this now? Perhaps because I have no choice but to listen. I suppose finally knowing why we're here can't make things any worse. 'They will be hard to find.'

I think about Pakoyai melting into the forest after a few steps.

'You said something before about—people being at risk, about warning them?' With nothing to distract me, other than the flies and mosquitoes, a fragment of conversation frees itself from somewhere in my head. 'You said...' But I can't seem to remember anything more.

Mum glances over at Maria.

'The area, the territory where they spend most time, is—is of interest to other people.'

What she says feels awkward. Almost rehearsed.

'What other people?' I ask.

Mum glances at Maria again—as if Maria is the one she doesn't want to tell. But Maria must know who the people are.

'Loggers,' she replies, reaching for the rest of her sandwich.

Maria and Pakoyai are silent, which is almost as strange as Mum's little speech.

'*Eu preciso ir,*' says Paulo, nodding in the direction of the boat.

He needs to leave, if he's going to get home before dark.

Paulo hugs everyone, then holds out his hand for me to shake.

'*Cuide deles.*'

Look after them.

I nod. I guess he doesn't know me very well.

As soon as Paulo has gone, Mum, Maria and Pakoyai begin strapping bags onto rucksacks with military efficiency.

I was expecting a lengthier briefing from Mum. More details about the *purpose* and *importance* of her work here. A few more clues at least. I feel a glimmer of frustration. Why do we need to keep rushing everywhere?

There is a loud rumble overhead, followed by a slow tapping sound, which speeds up until the taps begin to drown out the chirping chorus. Enormous raindrops splash from leaf to leaf, seeking the ground through a jigsaw of leaves.

'Put this on once you're wearing your rucksack.' Mum hands me a massive green poncho. I heave the rucksack onto my back. It's surprisingly heavy. Definitely not just my spare clothes and a toothbrush. When I pull the poncho on over the top, I'm glad it's so huge, billowing out like a tent rather than sticking to my skin.

'I should have given this to you before we left.' She passes me something small that looks like a smart watch. 'It has GPS.'

'GP—what?'

'GPS. It uses satellites to track your position. It's accurate to within one metre.'

'Don't you need to know where you are to begin with?' I ask, strapping it to my left wrist.

'I do know where we are. It also has tracking software so that you can see where I am in relation to where you are. In case anyone gets lost.'

'No one is getting lost,' calls Maria from somewhere within her poncho.

'The GPS is switched off for now. Battery life drops from two weeks to three days when it's tracking.'

Using her branch-broom, Pakoyai redistributes the layer of leaves and twigs.

In the space of a few minutes, we are ready to go, leaving no trace that we were ever here. I wonder why it matters when no one else will ever come this way.

'You follow Maria,' says Mum. 'I'll follow you, and Pakoyai will be at the back.'

It seems odd that Pakoyai will be last.

'*Vamos lá*,' says Maria, and without looking at a map, or her watch, she slips between the trees as if she's walking along the high street back home.

I gaze around at the forest which has swallowed us, mesmerized by the plant-explosion. Rotting logs and tree roots lurk beneath the carpet of leaves. I stumble, landing hard on my right knee. The bruise higher up my leg begins to throb.

'OK, Jackinho?' Maria calls softly.

Without turning round, she knew it was me who had tripped.

I focus on the ground a few metres ahead, glancing up with every screech and whoop from the dripping canopy.

I was expecting to hack my way through undergrowth. The forest looked impenetrable from the river. But it's not like that at all. There are leafy palms and ferns, but also massive moss-covered tree trunks soaring way above dozens of bendy-looking saplings.

Maria picks a route between them, occasionally pushing aside an extra-large palm leaf or stepping round a decaying trunk, barely changing her pace. It takes all my concentration to keep up.

We've been walking for an hour or so when the clouds lift. Damp earth steams in patches of dappled sunlight. The chirruping insects are so loud, I'm sure my head must be vibrating. We stop near the base of a tall tree to drink water and remove our ponchos. Once I've stuffed mine in the rucksack, mosquitoes whine around my head, settling on my shirt. I see now why Maria said we should wear long sleeves even though it's thirty degrees in the shade.

'We'll walk for another half an hour then we must stop, before it gets dark,' she says.

I am hot and sweaty, and starting to itch around my ankles and on my neck. I'm covered in new bites to match the ones on my hands. I want to stop now.

I guess the others are tired too. Maria isn't buzzing with her usual enthusiasm and Pakoyai has barely said a word since Mum's little speech earlier. Maybe they've realized how much I hate the forest, or how likely I am to mess things up—by accident, or intentionally.

When ten minutes have passed, Maria slows to a halt. I glance ahead, but the way seems clear. She's staring at something nearby. I peer through the leaves but see nothing, except the trunk of a very tall tree. Mum and Pakoyai have caught up and wait quietly behind me. They don't seem curious about why we've stopped.

I move closer and spot a strange shape near the base of the trunk—something wound around it in neat circles, resembling twenty or thirty enormous bracelets on a huge bark-covered arm. Perhaps it's a type of vine—but there's no way anything could have grown like that by itself. Someone has been here. Many times, judging by the number of loops. Protruding from the narrow gaps between the rings are feathers—yellow and orange, like soft flames licking at the trunk.

I turn to Pakoyai to ask her what it means—what the vine and the feathers are for. Who put them there? But the words die on my lips. Pakoyai is staring at the tree too, a tear rolling down her cheek.

She wipes her eyes and says quietly, 'It's a special place.'

Who has a special place in the middle of the rainforest?

Camp

'This is where we'll be sleeping,' says Maria.

I glance around. The ground is slightly flatter and with fewer tree roots, but otherwise no different to the rest of the rainforest. It must be a joke. But everyone seems busy, bustling about and preparing—for what? The arrival of a small cabin?

The tree with vines seems long forgotten.

Pakoyai has conjured another branch-broom and is sweeping the ground cover of leaves and sticks. Mum is clutching a long piece of cord.

'Hold this.' She passes me one end before I can say no, then ties hers to a slender trunk at about head height. 'Yours needs to be slightly lower.' She points to a small tree opposite hers, expecting me to secure it somehow. I don't have much choice, so

151

I wander over and tie several granny knots which seem to keep it in place, then watch uselessly as Mum stretches a poncho across the cord, making a kind of mid-air tent.

'OK, now you can hang the second one.' She hands me another piece of cord.

I suppose there's nothing else to do. While I search for suitable trees, she suspends two hammocks beneath her poncho.

'Bravo!' Maria calls from the edge of the clearing, where she is crouched next to a small stove with a saucepan balanced on top. The saucepan looks far too big for the stove. 'That should keep you dry and out of the way of snakes and scorpions. What more could you want, Jackinho?'

I don't know where to begin. I decide not to ask what we do if it starts raining before we get into bed, now that two of the ponchos have been converted into luxury accommodation.

Pakoyai has finished sweeping and is attaching a thick plastic bag to one corner of a poncho. She places a funnel in the top of the bag, and a sponge in the funnel, before realizing that I'm watching.

'To catch the rainwater,' she says. 'Minus the protein.' She points to the sponge. I frown, wondering what she means. Then without warning, a smile lifts the corners of my mouth. The sponge is to stop insects from washing into the bag with the rainwater. That's what she means by 'protein'. Pakoyai smiles back, and her whole face seems to shine.

It's so long since I've smiled. A real smile, not a puppet-master smile. It takes me by surprise. Especially since I don't understand why it happened.

'Food is ready!'

Maria has laid a poncho on the ground near the stove, for us to sit on. I don't know how I've made it this far through life without a poncho. They're so useful.

She passes me a bowl filled with rice, beans and vegetables. Somehow, she's prepared a meal on the floor of the rainforest. As I begin to eat, I realize how hungry I am.

'More?' She scrapes another spoonful from the pan for me and Pakoyai. When we've finished, she passes round strips of palm leaf. Pakoyai uses hers to wipe her bowl clean. I copy.

The light is fading. As the shadows grow deeper, I have a strange sensation that the trees are moving closer. It can't be very late—maybe six or seven p.m. Usually I'd be doing my homework or watching television, not thinking about going to bed, but the darkness is making me sleepy. I yawn, and glance towards the hammocks. They don't look very inviting.

'We go to sleep with the moon and rise with the sun,' says Maria, getting to her feet. 'And the sun rises pretty early.'

'Don't forget to check your boots before you put them on in the morning,' says Pakoyai. Perhaps it's my imagination, but her tone seems friendlier. 'You don't want a wandering spider to bite you on the toe—or anywhere, in fact.'

I brush my teeth, then clamber inside a hammock, letting myself sink into the fabric. Pakoyai and Maria are suspended either side of me. With the poncho overhead, it does feel similar to lying in a tent. When everyone is silent, I begin to notice the other noises. Distant branches snap. Closer to our camp, things rustle amongst the leaves. Claws scratch on bark. There is a snuffling sound directly beneath my hammock. I resist the urge to grab the head torch by my feet. Every muscle in my body is tensed, ready to move.

I'm not sure how long I lie like this. Pakoyai's breathing is slow and even, as if she's already asleep. I try to melt into the hammock again, and pick one noise to focus on. Not the mosquitoes. Maybe the frogs. Their low croaking is so constant, I barely notice it any more. Then I hear the gentle drip of rain on leaves. As it falls more steadily, the pitter-patter muffles every other sound.

My eyes begin to close. I think about the vines and the feathers, about who made the shapes... and why.

Invaders

'Pack everything away!' Mum shouts.

The canopy is shaking. Leaves swish back and forth. Debris showers the canvas above my head. Pakoyai and the others have untied their beds and are fiddling with the knots to the poncho.

There is a deafening roar, so low and so loud that I feel it in my bones.

'What was *that*?' I swing my legs to the ground and step into my trainers, hoping that nothing has crawled in during the night.

'Howler monkeys!' calls Maria, rolling up one of the ponchos. 'We're in their territory.'

'Should we run?'

Maria shakes her head. 'Their defence is to pooh all over our stuff.' The roaring belching noise is so loud I can barely hear her. 'And it's horrible.'

'It stinks!' Pakoyai holds her noise.

In the space of five minutes, the entire camp has been stuffed inside our rucksacks.

'Stand here, away from the main branches,' says Mum. 'If we keep still and quiet, they might leave us alone.'

After a few more minutes of tree shaking, there is an extra loud rumbling growl, like the loudest belch ever recorded. The rustling stops, and the monkeys swing off through the leaves as swiftly as they arrived. Yet even though the roars are further away, and further apart, they still drown out any other sounds.

'Loudest animal in the rainforest,' Mum says. I can't imagine anything louder, or a worse way to wake up. 'At least we can make an early start. Let's eat and get moving.'

Maria gives Pakoyai a bowl filled with squashed-looking rolls. 'Can you cut them in half while I peel the *tucuma*?'

Maria wasn't talking to me, but I reach over and take a handful of rolls, pulling them gently apart like Pakoyai.

Mum is by her rucksack, fiddling with one of the pockets. I wouldn't pay much attention, only there's something familiar in the way she's moving. As if she doesn't want to be seen. Each action is small and quick, she half-glances to see whether Pakoyai or Maria are watching. They're not. But I am. She takes out something square and black. It's thicker than her phone. She switches it on and off, handling it with care. For a few seconds she holds it up to her face and I realize it must be a camera. She never uses one at home. I didn't even know she had one. She slides it back inside a zip-pocket. For someone who wants to *share* and *talk things through*, she seems to have an awful lot of secrets.

Maria slips through the trees and I follow, but today feels different. I'm thinking less about mosquitoes and snakes, and more about why we're here. It seems a massive waste of time and effort just to warn a few families about something.

The air is slightly cooler, but an early start means hiking for longer. Perhaps long enough to find these people. But is it possible to locate anyone in the rainforest, if they don't really want to be found? I lose sight of Maria when she's only ten metres ahead.

I keep stumbling again, maybe because I'm tired. I try to pick my feet up, but I'm sore and achy from carrying a rucksack and from sleeping in the hammock, and even though I've been wearing trousers since we arrived, my legs are covered in bites.

I feel a tap on my shoulder.

'I saw you scratching. These will help.'

Resting in Pakoyai's palm are five or six shiny, dark green leaves.

'It's a natural repellent. Just rub them on your clothes.'

I'm covered in insect repellent, so I'm not sure what good a few leaves will do.

'Great. Thanks,' I reply.

A frown flashes across her face.

It's not my fault. I didn't ask her to be friendly. She wasn't before. Perhaps now she'll leave me alone again. But there's an uncomfortable feeling clawing its way from the greyness inside.

I didn't want to upset her.

I put the leaves in my pocket and keep walking.

We walk for several hours. The sun rises higher in the sky, and I begin to sweat. There is shade, but no breeze.

We pause only briefly, to eat. I try to remember which day it is. Thursday seems right. It's bizarre to imagine that last Thursday I was at school. In another week and a bit, I will be home again. For the thousandth time, I try to focus on how it will be when

I get back. How I will take charge. How I will be free to do things the way I want to. The way I need to. At home, I wouldn't worry about upsetting people.

I'm so absorbed in my train of thought, that I don't notice Maria has stopped. I almost walk straight into her.

She is crouched down, examining a large fragment of leaf, similar to the piece she gave us to clean our bowls, only inside this one something glistens—a sticky-looking substance.

Mum appears at my side.

'Honey,' says Maria, showing her the leaf. 'They passed this way. We should have a break, then walk in this direction.' She points to the right. 'We can make camp in half an hour or so.'

Mum nods.

I wonder whether I've missed something. Was there a message written on the leaf? Or did Maria figure out where to go from a smear of honey?

I thought they'd be excited, but it seems finding a clue to someone's whereabouts on a leaf in a forest with billions of other leaves is to be expected.

I lean against the tree, my rucksack cushioning me from the trunk. My back is unbearably hot, but I know that if I take my backpack off, I'll never put it on again.

The earth at the base of the trunk feels strangely spongy. I stamp my foot and it makes a dull thump, as if the ground beneath is hollow.

Seconds later, pain explodes in the back of my leg. It's so extreme that I collapse on one knee clutching at my calf. I hear myself groaning and Pakoyai shouting, 'Get him away! Pull him clear!'

I'm aware of being dragged a few metres across the forest floor, then Maria brushing down my clothes. Pakoyai takes off my shoes and socks. I have no idea what's going on and I don't care. I want the pain to stop. It pulses up and down my leg like hundreds of electric shocks. I feel my whole body beginning to shake.

'What's happened! What is it?' Mum cries.

Pakoyai has rolled up the bottom of my trousers, near where the pain began. She grabs a leaf and pulls something away from my leg, discarding it with the leaf, but the pain doesn't stop.

'Bullet ant,' she says calmly.

'A what?' Mum sounds panicked. She never sounds panicked.

'A bullet ant. I thought so but I had to check. It was attached to his sock,' she says, twisting my leg left and right. Maybe looking for more. 'There must have been a nest at the base of the tree.'

'An ant couldn't do this, could it?' Mum says quickly. She holds her water bottle close to my lips for me to take a sip, but I'm shaking too much.

'They have the most painful sting of any creature. That's why they're called bullet ants. When they sting, it feels like you've been shot.'

Maria unpacks the stove and starts heating water in the pan.

'I found these to help Jackinho,' she says. 'Matico leaves. They can ease the pain and the inflammation. I need to boil them.'

Mum nods. She seems a little calmer, and I'm glad, because I don't feel calm.

'When will it stop hurting?' My words come out jerkily, as if my teeth are chattering.

'I'm sorry, Jackinho, it's going to hurt for a while. You won't be going anywhere today,' says Maria.

'The ant was outside his sock,' says Pakoyai. 'Maybe he didn't get a full sting.'

I can't imagine how a full sting could be worse.

Maria looks up. 'OK, we'll make camp here so that Jack has somewhere to lie down. Then we can decide what to do.'

Just when I think the pain has eased, another wave begins.

Mum brushes the hair from my eyes. 'I'm so sorry, Jack,' she says.

I don't know if she means about the sting, or bringing me here, or both.

Pain

I'm aware of Maria and the others chatting, but I'm not really listening. I can't concentrate on anything except when the next wave of pain will arrive and how long it might last. I can't stop shaking either, as if I'm freezing cold—but I'm sweating. Pakoyai told me it was a side-effect of the bullet-ant poison. It feels like way more than a side-effect. The trees to which the hammock is tied are shaking gently too.

Mum ducks beneath the poncho.

'I wish there was something I could do.' She frowns, watching me shake. 'Jack, I don't think you'll be going anywhere tomorrow either. Pakoyai says that people call bullet ants, "twenty-four-hour ants", because that's how long the pain lasts.'

Why is she telling me this? Does she think it will make me feel better?

'She also said it might not last that long because the ant didn't give you a full sting. There's nothing to do except wait. Since we still have a few hours of daylight, Maria and I thought we should scout the area. She thinks several families might be camping near a tributary of the river a bit further north.'

Despite the pain, I feel annoyed. I'm clearly not OK and Mum is leaving. I guess that means Pakoyai will have to babysit.

'We won't be long,' Mum adds, slinging a small bag across her shoulder. She pauses, her hand resting on the bag. 'I should stay.'

I shake my head, at least I try to, but the shivering makes it look like I'm convulsing slightly. 'I don't need help.'

She watches me for a bit longer, then nods her head, before following Maria.

At least she didn't mention the medical kit, which probably had plenty of things to help with the pain and the shaking.

A new wave of electric-shock agony passes along my leg. It's exhausting.

Pakoyai gets to her feet. 'It's a while since you had the matico leaves. I'm going to find something else that will help.'

A few seconds later, she melts into the forest too.

I am completely alone.

Although I'm not. The forest around me is moving, alive with crawling, slithering, prowling things. I notice them less when I'm walking, or we're together eating. Now everyone has gone, I tune into the background percussion of croaking and chirping, punctuated by hoots and squawks.

If something crawled or slithered into my hammock now, I couldn't escape—not without help.

I become aware of a new noise, unlike the others. It's repetitive, with a harsh, steady rhythm unlike any animal's call. Almost like machinery. Perhaps my toxin-filled mind is playing tricks on me. I bet Pakoyai would know what it was. Probably some kind of bird.

I turn to the spot where she disappeared. She can't have been gone long. I need to calm down. I need to focus on something beyond the creeping crawling jungle.

My thoughts drift to Dad. Favourite memories float into my head. Dad watching me play at the inter-school football finals. It's raining and he is soaked but smiling. Now and then he claps, but he said it was important not to go crazy on the sidelines. Sometimes I wished he would go a tiny bit crazy though. I score the winning goal in the last two minutes of play, and he begins cheering and high-fiving the other parents one by one. I thought there could be no better feeling in the entire world.

The other memory is quite different. I'm sitting at the kitchen table, maths homework spread in front of me. It's algebra and I can't do it. I couldn't do the previous week's homework either and I'm worried that I'll be moved down a set. I've been staring at the same question for half an hour. Dad looks over my shoulder and frowns. He says that Mum is the brainy one and it's bad luck for me that I am stuck with him. He says I should take a break, do my other homework, then come back to maths. He disappears for an hour. When I reopen the maths books, he sits next to me, clutching several sheets of paper. We do the first question together. He gives me tips for the next one, then once I understand the method, he leaves me to it. Before he goes, I ask what's on the pieces of paper. They are printouts from a KS3 maths website. He has spent the last hour learning the basics of algebraic manipulation so that he could help me.

I replay the scenes, slowly. They usually follow the same sequence but sometimes I leave bits out, or linger on a favourite part, allowing the echo to soothe my thoughts.

These memories take away my uneasy feeling but, in their place, slips a strange emptiness. The echoes become hollow. There will never be any new memories.

I try again to picture Dad here, in the rainforest, but his face blurs, morphing into the face of someone I don't quite recognize. I reach in my pocket for the photo. I need to see him. As I unfold it, white flakes crumble into my hand. The image has curled into a roll of thin plastic; the paper beneath is dust. I stare at the pieces, trying to work out what's happened. I was wearing these trousers when I ran out into the rain. They were soaked, along with the rest of me. The photo must have got wet too, then dried out when Maria put my things in the oven. I've destroyed Dad's favourite photo. My favourite photo. My hands begin to shake again.

I squeeze my fist. Why did Mum have to bring me here? Why couldn't she stop working for two weeks. Is two weeks too much? The whirlwind stirs. I realize it's been still for the last few days, but now I feel it rising, gathering speed. A new wave of pain passes down my leg and the whirlwind slows, fading into the background again until it's spinning just out of sight, patiently waiting. For now.

There is the buzz of a rucksack zip. Pakoyai is back.

I peer beneath the poncho. She's holding a cup in one hand, and what looks like a bouquet of flowers in the other.

'Passion flower,' she says. Seeing my confusion, she adds, 'It helps with convulsions and with muscle pain, so it's good for you right now.'

She carries the cup over. 'What's that in *your* hand?'

Despite the heat, I feel my face flush. 'It's a photo.' She doesn't move. I don't have to explain what's happened to Pakoyai. It's none of her business. Yet I find myself saying, 'It's a photo of my dad. Well, it was. It's kind of fallen apart.'

She nods, her eyes fixed on my face as if she's trying to see straight through and into my thoughts.

'I understand,' she says. '*Saudade*.'

'*Sau*—what?'

'*Saudade*. It means...' For the first time since I met her, Pakoyai can't seem to find the right words.

'It means longing for something that cannot exist. For something other than the present.'

I stare back. She doesn't understand. She can't know how I'm feeling.

Only, she does.

Purpose

'There was a fresh palm frond den in the distance, near the river,' says Mum. 'Maria spotted it.'

'We'll go back first thing tomorrow,' adds Maria. 'To listen and to wait.'

They are fizzing with energy. Our small camp seems chaotic as they dart around, straightening and tidying, preparing for night. I wonder what they'll do—after they've listened and waited. Paulo will be back in two days, so we don't have long. There is no way I'm going to miss the boat home. Especially since my ant encounter.

They cook food and gather on a poncho to eat, but I have no appetite. I just want to sleep.

'Why don't you have a small portion?' Mum calls over.

I shake my head.

'Try to get some sleep then. I think you'll feel much better in the morning,' Maria says.

It's not even dusk, but the pain and shivering make me feel like one of the giant palm leaves, drooping beneath hours of relentless rainfall. Pakoyai's flower drink must have worked though, because the shaking has eased. My eyes begin to close.

Then I hear the noise again. The strange buzzing sound, like a motorbike, but very far away. Perhaps the bullet-ant poison has affected my hearing. I turn to look at the others. They are motionless, forks paused mid-air. Seconds later, Maria spoons a little more rice onto Pakoyai's plate. Mum has a sip of water. They carry on as if nothing happened, but it's too late. I noticed. They heard it too.

I open my eyes to a faint dawn glow. I slept through the night without waking. I've also stopped shaking. My lower leg aches, but the electric-shock pain has eased, and I really need the loo. I reach for one of my trainers and give it a good tap. I've learnt my lesson about rainforest insects. I duck beneath the edge of the poncho, then straighten up slowly, until I'm standing unaided for the first time in almost twenty-four hours.

It seems the rest of the forest has been awake for ages, or perhaps it never sleeps. Drips of water tap-tap softly on the leaves. Somewhere in the distance I recognize the whoop of a howler monkey. Birds call to each other in the canopy. My head spins as I gaze upwards, but the treetops are shrouded in a soft white mist. I take a few unsteady steps.

'Jackinho,' Maria calls softly, 'great to see you on your feet. I'm packing a few supplies for my trip with your mum. We'll be back around midday I hope, but it's hard to know, so we'll take food for dinner just in case. It rained in the night, so the water containers are all full. Oh,' she raises a finger in the air, 'before I forget—you need to activate the GPS tracking system on your watch. Then you can watch us walking round and round in circles.' She smiles her warm sparkly smile.

'Wow, you look awful!' says Pakoyai, rubbing sleep from her eyes as she wanders past, en route to Maria and the rucksacks.

'Thanks.' I try to sound annoyed but for some reason I'm not. Perhaps it's relief. I don't think Pakoyai would say I looked awful unless I seemed better.

Mum appears by my side.

'How are you feeling?'

'OK,' I say quietly.

Without warning, she gently takes my head in her hands. I try to shake her away, but it's impossible. She frowns as her eyes dart back and forth, assessing me for damage.

'Yes, I think you're on the mend,' she says, releasing me. 'You really need to eat though, darling.'

We gather on the poncho and share rice mixed with beans and a spicy yellow paste. My stomach doesn't seem to notice that this is not what I normally eat for breakfast.

I feel a little strength return, but my right leg still seems stiff and strange. I sit with it stretched out in front of me, avoiding pressure on the sting. It's obvious I can't go with Mum and Maria, but I don't want to spend all day stuck in my hammock listening to birds.

Maria hugs Pakoyai. '*Obrigada*,' she whispers.

Thank you. I wonder what Maria is thanking her for, then I realize. It's for staying behind with me. Again.

Mum isn't bustling about like Maria. For a second, I'm not sure where she is, then I spot her crouched near the backpacks.

'Right. I think we're ready,' she says, tucking the same piece of hair behind her ear several times and glancing around as if she might have forgotten something.

'OK, *amiga*, I'm ready,' Maria replies. She gives me and Pakoyai a little wave. 'See you soon.'

'Watch out for anything with six legs. Or any number of legs that isn't two,' says Mum. She never makes jokes with me, normally.

Perhaps in Mum's other life, there's another version of her too. Perhaps she's forgotten which version I am supposed to see.

I watch as they pick their way between low-growing palms, up a gentle incline. The canopy mist has evaporated and blades of dazzling sunlight slice between the trees. I hear the noise again. The unearthly growl. The weird, muffled engine sound. I have an urge to call out, to tell them to come back, to wait until we can go together, but they've disappeared. Melted into the rainforest once more.

I try to ignore the uneasy sensation growing in the pit of my stomach. To convince myself that it's another weird side-effect of the ant poison.

But it's not.

Pakoyai

Something taps me gently on the shoulder. I blink, trying to remember where I am. Pakoyai's dark brown eyes are fixed on mine. They sparkle like Maria's, even in the gloom beneath the poncho.

'You fell asleep soon after they left.' She passes me a cup. 'I thought maybe you should drink some water. It's really hot today.'

I take the cup and sit up, feeling disorientated.

'What time is it?'

'Just after ten. I'm going for a walk. I won't be long.'

The scent of banana and chocolate lingers in the humid air.

I take a few sips of water. I wonder where she's going. It's not as if there's a shop around the corner, or a somewhere else to be. But then, I wish I could leave the camp too. Everything in the rainforest seems to be busy, on the move. Except me.

I limp slowly around the swept area next to the hammocks, trying to judge how my leg is feeling. I ache all over, I guess from shivering and shaking, but the sting feels less sore.

I want to eat something which will give me energy. There's no way chocolate could survive here, but Maria has a packet of sweets stashed in her big rucksack. I saw her eating one yesterday. I open a few side pockets before locating the bag of orange-coloured toffees. I put one in my mouth. After a few minutes it's soft enough to chew. It doesn't taste of orange or toffee, but the flavour is familiar. Maybe it's *tucuma*. I'm reaching inside the bag for another, when a howler monkey screeches overhead. I snatch back my hand and stumble beneath the closest poncho. I'm in no mood for scraping stinking monkey pooh from my clothes. It screeches again, so close that I wonder whether it's in the camp. Do they attack people or just pooh on them? I lift the corner of the poncho. Perhaps I can throw something to scare it away.

Pakoyai is standing near the edge of the clearing. I beckon. She doesn't move. Surely she heard the cries too? I beckon more urgently, raising my arms and making an 'o' shape with my mouth, like a monkey. She lifts her fingertips to her mouth. At first I wonder whether she's frightened—then I see the crinkles round her eyes. She is smiling. I take a few steps and look around. There is no sign of a monkey and no noise from the trees either. Pakoyai is bent double, clutching her stomach, shaking with laughter. As I wait for her to stop, I realize that I am smiling too.

After a minute or so she fans her cheeks with her hands, wiping the tears from her eyes with the corner of her shirt. She takes a few deep breaths then lifts her chin, cupping her hands around her mouth to make an incredibly loud, barking cry.

Somehow, Pakoyai has learnt to copy the call of a howler monkey.

'That's amazing,' I gasp.

She grins. 'I can do others.'

She stands very still, then clicks her tongue, making a sound like a dolphin with a sore throat.

'Toucan,' she announces. 'One more.'

The last is a low whistling tune, similar to a slowed-down police siren.

'That was the purple-throated fruit crow. OK, now it's your turn.' She looks at me, a smile twitching the corners of her mouth.

I can't think of any animal noises. I feel ridiculous for failing on such a basic level. Weren't we taught animal sounds at nursery school?

'How about this.' I cup my hands around my mouth to appear professional, then make my best owl hoot—like Dad used to.

'That's really good!' Pakoyai claps. 'Another!'

I pause to think, then attempt a croaky sort of quack, but choke halfway through, so it sounds less like a quack and more as if I'm drowning. Pakoyai gives a thumbs down.

'Stick to the owl, Jackinho,' she says. 'Much better than your duck. Are you hungry? Maybe we should eat.'

I nod. 'I can help.'

'OK, *pato*,' she smiles.

I think that *pato* might be the word for duck.

There is a lightness within my chest. I like it, but I know it won't last.

'The others might be back soon. Can you check where they are?'

I fiddle around with the watch until I find the tracking screen. It's synced with both Mum and Maria's watches, but as they are together, their routes appear as a single jagged line.

'I don't think they've turned back yet.'

Pakoyai raises her eyebrows. 'They'll need to soon, or else it might be dark before they make it to camp. I guess that definitely means lunch for two, not four then.'

When we've finished eating, I take out the bag of sweets and pass one to Pakoyai. She's sitting between two pools of sunlight cascading between branches to the forest floor.

A pale blue butterfly, the size of two hands, flutters through the sunlight to rest on her arm. I smile. She looks like a Disney princess, or maybe Snow White. I didn't know butterflies could grow so big. Pakoyai seems completely unfazed, as if butterflies land on her all the time.

'It's tasting me,' Pakoyai mutters.

'Through its feet?' I joke.

'Yes. That's how butterflies taste.'

I assume she's teasing, but she's watching the butterfly, not me, as it turns a few circles, before fluttering away.

'How come you know so much about the rainforest. About plants and stuff?'

Pakoyai stares after the butterfly. When she turns round, she still seems focused on something in the distance, rather than on me.

'I learnt it from Mum,' she says. 'From Maria.'

'Is she an anthropologist?' I think about Mum's piles of books and shelves of artefacts. Maria's house is nothing like ours, and Maria seems nothing like Mum. Mum knows loads of stuff, but she's never taught me how to make toucan song, or howler monkey calls, or which plants help when you've been bitten by a bullet ant.

'No,' says Pakoyai. 'She's not an anthropologist.'

'Oh—an academic then, a professor?' Mum is both, but I'm sure that can't be essential.

Pakoyai shakes her head.

I feel as if I'm piecing together a puzzle but have no idea which parts are missing, or where to find them. How do Mum and Maria know each other? Mum says they are colleagues, but they live on opposite sides of the world—almost.

Pakoyai seems to know everything. I don't even know what Mum and Maria are doing here.

'So these families that they're looking for—if they find them, then will they come back with us?'

'No, definitely not.' There is a small, tight smile on her lips. I feel as if I've said something stupid. 'This is their home. But *invasores* have plans for the area.'

'Invaders?'

'Loggers.'

Loggers. They'd need more than a handsaw to cut down the trees in this forest. Perhaps all kinds of machinery. I think about the strange motorbike noises.

'But—there's so much rainforest—can't they just go to a different part, a part where there aren't any loggers?'

Pakoyai closes her eyes for a second, as if trying to calm herself.

'Just because they are nomadic, it doesn't mean they wander aimlessly around. Nomadic doesn't mean homeless. This whole area is their home.'

'OK, but I still don't understand why they've moved nearer to the loggers.'

'That's because you have a front door, and shop in a supermarket.'

I stare at Pakoyai blankly. Doesn't she have a front door and shop in a supermarket too?

'They are here,' she says slowly, 'because it's the time of year when fish spawn. They lay their eggs, then swim downstream. It's the perfect chance to catch lots of them without much effort, then smoke them and preserve them to eat later. These families have been doing it every year. For centuries.'

'I'm guessing—Maria told you?' I pause. 'But how does she know?' It's Mum's job to understand how

181

the natural world and people affect each other. But Pakoyai's already told me that's not what Maria does.

Pakoyai doesn't answer straight away. She looks up towards the tree canopy, her head tilted to one side.

Eventually, she says softly, 'Maria knows how they live because she is one of them.'

Puzzle

Pakoyai flits around the camp, washing bowls from lunch and sweeping the ground around the rucksacks. I watch her from the hammock, unable to move. I wanted to talk to her, ask her what she meant, but after we'd eaten, exhaustion defeated me.

It's the hottest day since we arrived in the rainforest. Too hot for sweeping. My back feels damp where it touches the fabric of the hammock. Sweat runs down my face. I wonder how Mum and Maria feel, trekking with their backpacks.

Thunder rolls in the distance. I jab at the buttons on my watch. The tracking screen now shows two jagged lines. One blue, one red. The blue line is heading back towards camp. The red line snakes off to the east. The uneasy feeling returns. Does that mean that Mum and Maria have separated? I think about mentioning it to Pakoyai, but there's bound to be an obvious explanation, one which makes me seem stupid.

The saplings at either end of the poncho rustle gently as Pakoyai climbs into her hammock, clutching a thin book. Who brings a book to the jungle?

I shuffle round onto my side, so that I'm facing her.

'What did you mean?'

Pakoyai's head jerks up in surprise.

Despite the background chirping and croaking, my voice sounds unnaturally loud. I start again, more softly.

'What did you mean when you said *she's one of them?*'

Pakoyai rests the book on her chest.

'Mum hasn't always lived in the city. She was born here.' She pauses. 'They are her family. Her people.'

'Here?' I frown. 'In the rainforest?'

'Not just in the rainforest, but in this part. Where her parents lived too.'

My brain is whirring. Coming here from the city felt like stepping onto Mars. Would it feel the same in reverse? Maria was born here, her people are here. Yet she lives in the city now.

'But she doesn't live here any more.' I'm thinking aloud because there doesn't seem to be space for all the thoughts inside my head. 'Why did she leave?' I ask quietly.

Pakoyai lies very still. I think she is about to answer, when there is a soft thud from somewhere nearby. We both sit up.

The edge of Pakoyai's poncho lifts and Maria's face appears.

'Olá,' she smiles. 'Jackinho, you look soooo good! A big improvement on yesterday, no?'

I nod.

She glances around. 'Where is Sofia?'

Pakoyai turns to me.

I shrug, checking Maria's face for signs that she might be playing some kind of trick. But her smile has vanished.

'That's strange, because she left before me.'

She lets the poncho drop, and I hear the soft pad of her feet as she walks to and fro outside, perhaps making sure that we aren't the ones playing a trick.

I pull on my trainers. My whole body feels stiff, as I walk slowly over to join her. She is by the rucksacks now, scanning the forest left and right, but stops as soon as she sees me coming.

'I'm sure there's a good explanation,' she says. 'You know your mum, always wanting to investigate everything. Perhaps she spotted a new bird or a special flower on her way back.'

Perhaps I don't know Mum as well as Maria thinks. But one thing is certain. She's not here, and Maria is worried.

Lost

Maria paces back and forth.

'I shouldn't have let her go on ahead,' she says, half to herself. She glances towards me. 'But I'm sure she's fine. We've trekked here before. Our trail was fresh.'

My head is spinning. Minutes ago, Pakoyai told me that Maria had grown up right here, in the rainforest. Then Maria returned from her trek, without Mum. Now, she says they separated, and she has no idea where Mum might be.

Instinct makes me want to grab my rucksack and look for her, but for once I accept that running off isn't going to help. Besides, I can barely walk.

I try to think what Dad would do. If I was panicking about schoolwork, or we'd lost a big football match. If things went wrong, how did he fix them? Talking always seemed to stop my head spinning. He would talk to me.

'Did you find them?' I mutter.

Maria stops pacing. 'What's that, Jackinho?'

'Did you find them—the people you were looking for?'

She perches next to me on the poncho.

'Not exactly.' She shakes her head.

I frown, not sure that I understand. 'But—how can you not know?' My leg aches, so I stretch it out in front of me.

Maria smiles, but it doesn't reach her eyes. 'I made contact with one of the hunters. He wasn't much older than you. We hadn't spoken before, but he knew about me.' She smiles again—her half-smile.

'Did you sit down together, like this?' I nod towards Maria and Pakoyai, perched opposite me.

'No. We didn't get this close. The risk of passing on a virus to which he had no immunity was too great. But we talked about the *invasores*. Often a few loggers creep in and fell one of the ancient hardwood trees—a rosewood or a jatoba. Then they creep away again, dragging the timber with them. But my people don't need me to tell them that trees are disappearing. Trees which take decades to grow.'

I'm not sure if sitting here will help to find Mum, but already my head feels less like it's about to explode.

'Then why make all this effort—the boat, the trekking?'

'Because this time it's different. There are many valuable trees here, including a lot of mahogany—the most valuable of all. I heard that the loggers had brought machinery on barges. Machinery for cutting down more than a few trees. The narrow trails will turn into a road. A few trees will turn into many. Then, when everything valuable has gone, people will say there's nothing special here, why not let the farmers clear the area—at first the size of one football pitch, then two...'

I glance around at the palms and vines, at fat tree trunks rising up to the canopy, branches draped with moss-like stuff. It doesn't seem possible that this could ever be just a field.

Maria sighs, throwing a hand in the air as if tossing something away. 'And if there's so much profit to be made, they won't let a few families stand in their way. The loggers will stop at nothing. I don't think I was convincing, though. I've come with warnings before. The families are sick of moving away from parts of the forest which are their home. Moving from here would mean losing the best fishing area—one they've used for hundreds of years. Why should they go? Where should they go?'

Pakoyai has been listening quietly. Now, she leans over, placing a hand on Maria's arm. 'You did your best, Mãe.'

Maria closes her eyes and takes a deep breath.

Everything Maria has said, everything Pakoyai told me, twists and turns in my mind. I have more pieces of the puzzle, but it's incomplete. In fact, the more pieces I am given, the larger it grows. Questions swirl, just out of reach. Maria was born here. She knows the families, the people. She heard about what the loggers were doing. Her reasons for coming are clear to me. But why did she leave in the first place? As for Mum—why did she come? Why is this trip so important to her?

Where is she?

'I'll check the GPS tracker again,' I murmur.

'Yes!' Maria says.

Why didn't I think of it before?

Thunder rolls again, closer this time. Raindrops patter in the canopy. Seconds later, a few fat drops splash onto the leaves next to me. Maria drapes the poncho we've been sitting on over the backpacks.

We huddle beneath the other two, suspended from the trees. It's harder to see my watch display in the gloom. But I can make out that one line has snaked all the way back to camp. The other, which went off to the right, hasn't moved.

Maria stares at the lines, trying to make sense of what she's seeing.

'So this one is mine?'

'Yes, the blue one.'

'And this red one is Sofia?'

I nod.

'Oh no.'

Maria is staring at the watch, one hand clasped over her mouth.

'What?' I ask. A cold sensation trickles along my spine, even though I'm sweating.

'Mãe?' says Pakoyai.

'*E se ela entrou na área onde estão os invasores?*' whispers Maria.

'No.' Pakoyai shakes her head.

I feel like shouting at them to stop. Stop talking to each other and talk to me.

'What is it?' I ask, my eyes flicking from Maria to Pakoyai. 'Tell me.' The rain is falling harder, pattering above our heads and dripping from the edge of the ponchos.

'Mãe—Maria—thinks that Sofia could have wandered into the area where the loggers are working.'

'Is that bad?' I ask.

Pakoyai hesitates. 'What they're doing is illegal. They don't want anyone to see. Anyone who might tell others.'

'But someone has already seen, somebody warned Maria. They'd spotted the barges. It's not exactly a secret.'

'Yes,' says Maria quietly. 'But it was only word of mouth. I trusted the people who told me, but why would anyone else—without proper evidence? Without information about exactly where it was happening? That's what the loggers want to keep secret.'

'But—what if she was just looking for a plant, or following an animal, like you said? Maybe her watch has run out of battery and isn't showing her true location. She might be on her way back already—or almost here.'

Maria nods slowly. 'Yes, Jackinho, you are right.' She rubs her forehead with her hand. 'I overreacted.' She glances at Pakoyai when she says this. 'So, I will go back along the trail to meet her. She has a compass and a whistle. Your mother is an experienced trekker.'

'But, Mãe, won't it be dark soon? You can't trek in the dark—no one can,' says Pakoyai.

'I won't go far.' Maria looks at me and shakes her head. 'The chances of getting lost in the dark are infinitely greater than during daylight—even for me. Your mother knows this too. If she hasn't returned before nightfall, she will find a good place to wait for sunrise. In the rainforest, dawn always arrives early, you know.' She gives me a small smile, then heads out into the rain.

I watch as Maria tugs a poncho—the fourth poncho—from the top of her rucksack.

That means wherever she is, Mum has nothing to shelter her from the never-ending rain.

I picture her alone, soaked, and have the strangest sensation that I'm falling, with no way to stop. My family is disappearing and I can't stop that either.

First Dad.

Now Mum.

Fall

'Come on, help me with the stove.' Pakoyai passes me the tiny tripod, then empties the contents of several packets into a pan. 'Let's get something ready for when they return. Can you reattach those bags too?' She points to the water reservoirs, dangling from a nearby tree. 'We should collect as much as we can.'

It takes me several attempts to secure the first one without any gaps. It's hard to see in the dusk light. Hard to concentrate too.

Maria has been gone for over an hour. For the first ten minutes, I watched the blue line as it snaked away, then I stopped checking. I didn't like to see the red line—unmoving.

'Mãe?' Pakoyai gets to her feet, dropping a spoon into the bubbling pan.

I throw the piece of cord I'm clutching onto a

hammock and follow her gaze. Maria is approaching the edge of the clearing, pushing strands of wet hair from her forehead. She is alone.

The falling sensation rushes up. I clutch at the smooth branches of a sapling.

'Jack? Jackinho?'

Maria's voice pulls me back. I try to focus on the smell of food cooking, on the sound of rain dripping. Anything to keep me from disappearing down and down, with no way of stopping.

'Jack, I didn't find her, but the light was bad, and if she has any sense she will have stopped somewhere already.'

Maria's voice has a soothing edge, but it feels as if she's trying to reassure herself, as much as me.

'The rainforest is dangerous for those who don't respect it.' Pakoyai looks up from the narrow space between the hammocks. The only dry area for cooking. 'Your mum respects the forest.'

'She's right.' Maria appears at my side. 'I didn't find her, but your mother has the most important quality for survival. Common sense. It's late,' she says firmly. 'Let's eat, let's rest, and then at first light, I will find her.'

I glance at Mum's empty hammock.

'*We* will find her,' I say.

Follow

I lie awake, filling my head with versions of the kaleidoscope face painting I saw when we left the city—different colours, different features. Patterns swirl but do not calm my thoughts. I imagine what Dad would say if he knew Mum was missing. I picture myself telling him how she tricked me into this trip. How she doesn't care. I can't make out his features, but I see him shake his head. But if this isn't her fault, if I can't blame Mum, then who? If I don't find an answer, the swirling darkness might swallow me up.

Halfway through the night, the rain ceases and the chirruping frogs grow louder. I don't tune into the forest noises so much now. I'm starting to realize that the worst things often make no sound at all.

A faint glow illuminates the pale mist, drifting below the canopy.

Maria stirs. She sits up and rubs her eyes.

'Still feeling strong enough to come?' she says softly. 'I can't carry you back if you start to feel bad,' she adds.

'I feel OK,' I say.

'I think we should leave some things here,' says Maria. 'Then if Sofia comes back via a different route, she will know that she's found the right place. She'll wait for us.'

We untie, fold and squash things into the rucksacks, then eat dry biscuits and sip water.

Ten minutes after waking, we are ready to go.

'The battery on my watch is low,' says Maria. 'I'm going to turn it off for now. How much do you two have?'

'Half,' I reply.

'Almost full,' says Pakoyai.

'OK. Pakoyai, turn yours off and we'll use Jack's until it runs out.'

I'm glad. I don't want to look at mine, but turning it off would feel like cutting an invisible thread.

Maria leads the way. The trail is easy to follow. A subtle flattening of the ground indicates where her feet—and Mum's—have trodden before. Even so, I struggle to keep up. My body feels as if I went for a long run yesterday. Possibly a marathon. My muscles are tired and achy, but I'm worried that if I go slowly, Maria will decide I'm not fit enough to come.

She must know, because after twenty minutes or so, she suggests we stop for a drink.

While we pause, I stay well away from the base of any large trees, copying Maria as she rests on her haunches, hands on her knees.

We apply more insect repellent, then keep going. I reassure myself that little time has passed since Mum walked the same route—less than twenty-four hours.

Raindrops sparkle on the broad leaves. The forest smells of flowers and earth. It seems safe and enticing. I understand why people come here unprepared.

Despite the roots and obstacles, I barely glance down. I don't want to miss the first glimpse of Mum. I wonder how she'll look after a night sheltered beneath palm bushes. Tired. Grumpy. Dad used to say that Mum could look great in a paper bag. I would make retching sounds.

After an hour or so, the aching and stiffness improve. Maybe the ant poison has finally left my body.

Maria stops again, waiting for us to draw level. 'Jackinho, may I look at your watch? I don't want to miss the point where Sofia left this trail. It will be much easier if we're able to follow her exact route.'

I hold out my wrist.

Maria nods. 'OK. I think it will take another hour to reach it, then maybe the same again to arrive at the place where her tracker stopped. But I'm assuming we'll meet her along the way.' She smiles weakly. 'Her tracker still hasn't moved.'

Dappled sunlight filters to the forest floor and I feel the temperature rise. Once more, I focus on the trail. That way, when Mum does appear, it will be a surprise. If you'd spent the night sheltering beneath a tree, surely you would want to head back to camp at first light? By that logic, we should have met halfway. But halfway has been and gone. I find myself straining to hear the faint trill of a whistle, or someone's voice.

Our camp made the jungle seem small. It was the centre from which everything radiated. Now the poncho and hammocks are far behind us, consumed by the forest, no more significant than the leaves on the trees. Less than a needle in a haystack. A thousand haystacks. I feel as if the forest might have consumed Mum too. I focus on Maria's blue rucksack, on the birdsong, anything to stop me from falling, down and down again.

Maria checks my watch. She walks more slowly, studying the ground as she goes. Several times she pauses, taking a few steps to the left or right, before rejoining the trail.

A few minutes later she pauses again. 'Wait here.'

She passes through a grove of saplings, examining the branches at around shoulder height.

'I think this is it,' she calls. 'I think this is the route Sofia took. I can't be one hundred per cent sure, but someone came this way—someone wearing boots, rather than barefoot. Let's have a snack, then keep going.'

'Have one of these.' Pakoyai passes me a yellow-ish rectangular biscuit. I ate one yesterday. It was tasteless, but filling.

We eat in silence. Maria doesn't mention finding Mum, or why we haven't yet.

Then it starts. The noise. The engine sound. It's much closer.

Maria jumps up.

There is no doubt that we've all heard it this time. Maria's eyes are wide. Not with surprise, or confusion, but with fear.

Fear

The trail takes us downhill. Vegetation is denser here. Birdsong echoes. Maria checks my watch so frequently that I unclip it and give it to her.

'We've reached the point where Sofia's trail ends on the tracker. We can keep going in this direction, or...' She hesitates.

At first I wonder why—then I realize. She doesn't have another plan.

Maria shakes her head, taking a slow breath in and out. 'Jackinho, I thought we'd find her by now. That our paths would cross, or that if she'd become disorientated, she would stay put, blow her whistle and wait.'

We stand in silence. The rainforest carries on chirping and howling. Life goes on around us, oblivious.

My mind scrabbles for options. Something to focus on to stop me from falling.

'What if she got lost and *didn't* stay put? Perhaps *we* should stay in the same place for a while, instead? If we're all on the move, there's far less chance of our paths crossing.'

Pakoyai is staring at me intently. 'Or perhaps she just took a different route back, and didn't think to blow her whistle because she knew where she was going?'

I nod.

'OK,' Maria says, sounding more confident. 'It's still early, so perhaps we carry on for twenty minutes? If we don't find Sofia, then we head back to where the trails diverged, and wait. We blow the whistles every few minutes. If we have no luck, then we head to camp to see if she's there. What do you think?'

I hesitate, worried about making the wrong decision. That by picking one plan over another, we could miss Mum by five minutes—or fifty metres.

'I think it sounds good,' Pakoyai says in a decisive tone that would have annoyed me a few days ago. Now I understand that she isn't trying to take over. She's trying to help.

I nod again—not sure that my voice will sound as confident as hers.

'Is your leg all right, Jackinho?' Maria asks. 'I keep forgetting to check—you're doing so well.'

'It's fine,' I say, even though it's not. My leg is throbbing, and I feel weak.

'Then let's keep moving. First though, a little more of this.' She holds up the bottle of insect repellent. 'We're getting close to the river. There'll be even more insects trying to bite you.'

I lift the spray, then freeze. I hear shouting. It's definitely not a howler monkey. It's a man's voice.

Pakoyai freezes too.

'We have to get out of here,' Maria whispers. 'Now.' Her fingers close around the rucksack straps. Silently, she swings it onto her back.

'How do you know it's not the families you were looking for? Weren't they by the river?' I say softly.

'It's not them,' Maria says, shaking her head firmly. 'They have other ways of communicating in the forest.'

The pieces of the puzzle slide back and forth in my head.

'It's the loggers, Jack,' says Pakoyai.

'But—what if they know something? They might have seen Mum.'

Maria is staring at me, eyes wide. 'Were you not listening before? That's exactly what I was afraid of, Jack. We have to hope that Sofia heard them too. That she did what is sensible.'

'What's that?' I ask.

'She ran,' says Maria, her voice barely audible.

One piece of puzzle begins to lock into place. She couldn't have come *this* far by accident. No. Mum came here intentionally. For some reason, I think she came *looking* for the loggers.

'Maria,' I say slowly. She looks at me, her eyes still wide. 'May I have my watch?'

'Why, Jackinho?' She tries to unclip it, but her hand is trembling and she can't lift the clasp.

'I need to go further. Will you come with me?'

'No, please, Jack,' Maria pleads.

'I can't turn back now.'

Pakoyai is silent. Perhaps she can tell that my mind is made up.

'Jack, if they see you then—'

'Then what?' I feel as if another piece of puzzle might be within my reach.

Maria shakes her head.

'You don't know what you're doing,' Pakoyai mutters. 'You don't understand.'

'I wish I did,' I reply. 'I won't go far. I just...' I can't put my feelings into words. 'I won't go far,' I repeat.

I take a few steps down the hill, towards the voices.

I keep my body low and walk as silently as I can. Without Maria to follow, I must concentrate harder on where to put my feet amongst the branches and rotting leaves.

After a few minutes, I pause to wipe sweat from my forehead. It felt like there was no choice but to carry on, but perhaps what I'm doing is no different to running from Maria's house in the rain. Reckless.

I stare through the endless layers of green and brown, wondering whether I should turn back, when I hear voices again. Instinctively, I crouch down, peering between the trees. The foliage is so dense it's impossible to see far. Instead, something closer catches my eye. A flash of turquoise. Pakoyai warned me about poison dart frogs, how the toxins on their skin are so powerful that just one touch can kill. I lean cautiously towards the bright flash, but it's not a poison dart frog. It's Mum's headband.

My heart hammers in my chest. I lift the headband gently from the end of the branch. It has a faint flowery scent. My mouth feels dry. Mum was here. Perhaps in the very spot where I'm standing. I close my fingers around the soft cotton, as if that might release the secret of where she is now.

Dad and I misplace things. Lose them. Mum doesn't. She would notice if her headband slipped off. She would pick it up.

I let the chirruping, rustling percussion wash over me as I try to think. Was she running? Was someone chasing her, and the headband came off as she ducked beneath the bush?

Behind me, leaves rustle. I snap my head round. Maria and Pakoyai are coming.

'We couldn't let you go alone,' Maria whispers. She attempts a smile, but her face is tight with fear.

'What's that?' Pakoyai glances at my hand.

Maria gasps. 'Sofia's?' I nod. 'Where did you find it?'

I point. 'Hanging from that branch.'

Maria steps closer, examining the branch and the ground beneath.

'I think she was running—trying to get away from something, and it got caught,' I say.

Maria nods her head slowly. 'Perhaps.'

I feel my chest tighten.

'What if—' I start to speak, but no more words will come. I take a few breaths, then try again. 'Do you think the loggers might have taken her and left this as a warning—a sign?' I hold out the headband.

'Loggers aren't subtle,' says Maria. 'That's not the kind of sign they would leave.'

I take a few steps further down the hill.

'Jack, stop!' Maria hisses. 'Going further is not going to help Sofia.'

Maria can't know that, but I stop anyway. I am watching Pakoyai reach for an object in the leaf litter. She has her back to me, but I can see it resting in the palm of her hand. Why hasn't she beckoned us over to look? I move closer. She doesn't turn round. She doesn't move at all. In her hand, is a clump of moss. On the moss is something brownish-red.

Without Pakoyai telling me, I know that it's blood.

The falling sensation swoops, overwhelming me. I sink to my knees, trying to steady myself.

I hear someone whispering my name over and over.

'Jack, Jackinho.' I turn my head to look at Maria. Her eyes glisten. 'We must not give up, Jackinho.'

I am vaguely aware of Pakoyai nearby, treading softly amongst the leaves. I know that she is scouting for more clues. For answers.

My breathing slows. I wipe the sweat from my face. I need to do something. Before I can get to my feet, Pakoyai walks swiftly towards us.

'Look.' She passes Maria a crimson feather. 'Toucan,' she adds.

Maria holds the feather in her fingertips.

'They've been here too,' she whispers.

'The loggers?' I ask. The falling sensation lingers.

'Not the loggers. My people. Do you remember the place we passed on our first day here? The special place?'

'No,' I say shakily. 'What special place?' I want real answers. Not riddles.

'The tree,' says Pakoyai.

I do remember. The vine coiled carefully around the trunk. Feathers like flames.

'Those feathers are a sign. A connection. They mark the spot where something happened. Something important.'

I stare at the fluffy red object in her hand, trying to believe it might have been left here on purpose.

'Aren't there thousands of toucan feathers lying around the forest?'

'I know this forest. Toucans don't nest here, in this valley.'

'But the blood—' I begin.

'Someone has been hurt, but not by my people.'

I try to concentrate on what Maria is saying. My head is spinning again.

'So who did they leave the feather for? To show what? How do we know Mum isn't—' I close my eyes. 'How do we know she's alive?'

'Jackinho, I don't know, but finding this feather so close to Sofia's headband gives me hope. Hope that she might be OK.'

'I will show you where I found the moss,' Pakoyai says to Maria. 'See if we can pick up Sofia's trail from here. At least work out which direction she went in.'

Maria nods. 'Yes, Pakoyai, *querida*,' She places her hand on Pakoyai's shoulder. 'So calm and smart.' She pauses for a second then says, 'Your father would have been very proud of you.'

At first, I think Maria is talking to me, but she's still looking at Pakoyai.

Her words pull me back to the forest. To the present. Towards another piece of the puzzle.

'The tree,' Pakoyai and Maria both turn to look at me, 'the feather tree. You said it was special. Why?'

'We really need to leave,' Maria whispers. 'We're in danger here.'

'Not until you tell me why,' I say quietly.

'OK, Jackinho,' Maria murmurs. 'OK. A long time ago,' she says slowly, picking her words with care, 'some of my people were camping near that tree, hunting. There were loggers then too. Different loggers, but same ideas. There were valuable trees they wanted, and the hunters made them nervous. One day they decided enough was enough. The hunters had to go. The loggers went after the first family they found. The family ran. A little girl escaped, but not the mother and father.' She takes a deep breath. 'I was the little girl. The mother and father were my parents.'

Courage

I stare at the piece of turquoise fabric in my hand. At the feather in Maria's.

'Where did you go?' I ask softly. 'After you had escaped.'

'I kept running and running,' Maria says, 'until I had no idea where I was. After a day or so, I found the river. I was very hungry. Some fishermen paddled me to the nearest town and one of the families took me in.'

Maria ran and kept running, but she was running for her life.

'Does Mum know—your story?'

Maria nods. 'We've known each other a long time. We met when she came to my research institute. I was studying rainforest ecosystems, but she wanted to talk about my campaigns to protect the families who lived there instead. People often see them as two separate things, but your mother was like me. She felt that you cannot destroy one without ripping the heart from the other. She also knew how to raise awareness. What people needed to see, to hear. Who to contact. She wanted photos, evidence, but I said it was too dangerous.' Maria rests her forehead in her hand. 'Jack, it's time to go. Sofia needs us, wherever she is. She may be injured and wounds become infected quickly in the jungle.'

Maria and Pakoyai head towards the spot where Pakoyai found the moss. Slowly and methodically, they scan the surrounding earth, gradually moving further and further in the direction from which we came.

I brush the dirt from my knees, and begin to follow, when voices echo up the hill. Men's voices, growing louder. Someone is coming this way. The voices stop. Seconds later, there is shouting.

'*Eu estou vendo eles! Ali!*'

I hear branches snap, then the swish of feet running through the leaves.

'*Ali!*'

Pakoyai and Maria seem rooted to the forest floor, staring open-mouthed towards the voices.

Seconds later, a figure bursts through the under-growth a few metres to my right. Two more figures push through the bushes, pointing and shouting. Not at me. They're pointing at Maria and Pakoyai.

Pakoyai runs a few steps, but Maria seems unable to move.

'Mãe! *Invasores!*' Pakoyai screams.

Her voice seems to penetrate Maria's trance. She takes a sharp breath in, then turns to follow Pakoyai. One of the men grabs at Maria's rucksack, but she jerks free, ducking below a branch that he has to sidestep.

Maria and Pakoyai dart nimbly round trees and over tree stumps. The three men stumble after them, shouting, but not gaining on them.

My heart is pounding. I realize that I've been holding my breath. I take a few gulps of damp air, then begin to follow. My leg hurts. It's stiff and aching from the walk here. Pain shoots along the back of my calf. I stumble, then pause. How can I possibly outrun those men? There is no way I could dart through the trees like Maria and Pakoyai. Right now, I'm not sure I can move more than a few steps.

I realize that I can't hear shouting. The forest is eerily quiet. Does that mean that Maria and Pakoyai have been captured? Or that they've run so far that they are out of earshot?

I strain to make out any sound that might give me a clue.

There are voices again. Getting louder. Moving quickly. Angry voices heading this way, perhaps faster than if they were dragging people against their will. I feel a flash of hope. Then my chest tightens as I realize I am standing in full view, and cannot run. The men sound close enough to see me through the foliage at any second.

I am frozen, like Maria.

My fingers tighten around Mum's headband. If I am caught, then who will help her?

I drop to the ground, and start crawling towards the tree, next to where I found the headband. I wince as my hand presses down on a thorn. The foliage is thicker near the ground, and crouched down, I am wider. I throw myself behind the trunk as the men draw so close, I can make out every word.

They're not going to tell Bernado. He will go nuts. They will say something about a false alarm. They're going to check the area, just to make sure.

My heart thumps. I lift my head a little, the tree is very wide, but if they peer round the side, they will see me. Near the base, the bark seems to change colour. It's darker. I try to focus on the darker patch and realize that it's not bark at all, but a hole, a hollow.

I have no time to wonder whether an animal discovered it first, and is living inside. I slip off my backpack and wriggle through the gap. My shoulders scrape the top, but the hollow is larger than the entrance. High enough for me to sit upright. I pull my rucksack in by the straps and squash it in front of my knees. I try to keep still, but my chest is heaving, my breath echoing in rasping gasps. There is a noise just outside. I press myself into the curve of the tree. I'm out of sight, but if they look inside, it will be impossible for me to escape. I try to reassure myself that you cannot see the hollow unless you are lying on the ground, like I was.

One of the men shouts, '*Pare!*'

There is silence.

I picture them turning slowly round, scanning the undergrowth for movement. I imagine them spotting the large tree, walking closer to investigate.

I close my eyes. My heart feels as if it might burst through my chest. I have no idea how much time is passing. Seconds. Minutes.

There is a soft rustle of leaves by the entrance, then a flash of movement as a small brown bird darts away. I stop myself from crying out, but the urge to look through the gap is almost unbearable.

I hear voices moving away, down the hill. I wait for my heart to slow. Have they decided Maria and Pakoyai were alone? I need to leave. To get as far away as possible. As I lean towards the entrance, there is a shout from only metres away.

'*Estou indo também!*'

One of the men had stayed behind. Waiting to see if anyone would break cover. Footsteps crunch past.

I count to sixty, slowly. Then lean forwards, but before I crawl through the gap, something catches my eye, something glinting in the gloom of the hollow. Perhaps it's a small creature's eyes. Impulsively, I reach out my hand, ready for sharp teeth to sink into my fingers. Instead they close around something smooth. I hold it up to the light. It's Mum's watch.

I stare at the shiny black surface, trying to figure out why it's here.

A few minutes pass. I clip the watch to my wrist. Somehow it makes me feel closer to Mum.

I press the 'On' button. The screen lights up. The battery hasn't run flat. Which seems strange.

First the headband, now the watch.

The headband makes sense, but why is her watch *here*? Did someone take it from her?

I'm missing something obvious. But I'm too tired to figure out what.

You would only turn your watch off if you were planning to use it later.

Maria said that Mum wouldn't try to trek in the dark. She had no poncho. She needed somewhere to shelter.

She was sheltering here. She was in this hollow. Sitting exactly where I am sitting.

Was she frightened? Was she in pain? Why didn't she take the watch with her? My heart slows a little, replaced with a different sensation, like homesickness.

It seems ridiculous that we have both occupied this same tiny space, yet she has gone, and I have no idea where she is, or what's happened to her.

I need to go too. Maria still has my watch, but I can use Mum's to retrace the trail. I can make it back to camp. Get help. Somehow.

Now that my eyes have adjusted to the dark, I take one more look around the hollow. Near where I saw Mum's watch, is another object. It has an angular shape which doesn't fit amongst the decaying wood. I lean a little closer. It's her camera.

I turn it over in my hand. Why did she take it with her on the trek? Why did she leave it here? There's a screen on the back and a disc on the other side. When I switch it on, the disc unfurls like a telescope. Above the screen is a small window. I hold the camera up to my face and look through the window. As I move the camera around, the disc zooms in and out. I press the 'mountain' symbol, and a picture gallery appears.

I tab through the pictures, but they're so blurry it's hard to work out what they are. I tab through again, more slowly. One photo might be of a truck, another of some figures, but I can't see the people's faces. Mum must have been moving when she took them.

Then I realize. They are pictures of the loggers. That's why she was here. That's what she was doing. She was here to take pictures of the loggers. To gather evidence. It's the reason she came. The reason she was hurt, or worse.

I rub my leg. Mum won't have been happy with the images she got. A few blurry photos aren't enough to show what's happening. Who is doing it.

My palms are sweating. If she wasn't able to gather evidence, who will? I know what I have to do. It's not the first time I've done something reckless. But this time I am frightened.

I think about what will happen if the loggers see me. I wonder if they have guns. If they chase me, I won't be able to outrun them. I feel my breath quicken.

I crawl backwards, out of the hole, blinking in the daylight. There is no sign of the men. Broken branches and flattened ground are the only clues that they were here at all.

I decide to leave my rucksack in the hollow. It's hard to stay low or duck under branches with something on your back. Clutching the camera, I take a deep breath and pick my way down the hill. Every step taking me further from the camp, further from the trail. Further from safety.

My feet make a noise however carefully I place them. After a minute or so, I stop and listen. There are no voices, no machines. About fifty metres ahead, the forest floor is bathed in sunlight. Trees and foliage have been cut away, creating a huge clearing. I crouch down. There's no one around. To the right, a large object is tucked behind the few remaining palms. I hold the camera to my eye and gently press the button on top. It zooms in to show a small digger, and beyond that, a truck, its flat trailer loaded with timber. I take a few pictures, but they're not very clear. I need to get closer, but every step I take towards the clearing, makes it less likely I will be able to escape.

I loop round to the right, towards the far side of the vehicles, my heart pounding. I have a clear shot of the timber on the truck, and an area of forest the size of our school playground which has already been cleared. I take pictures of the number plates and the narrow track heading up from the river. The loggers must be taking a break or doing something down by the river. I'm sliding the camera into my pocket, when a man appears in the clearing. He is scowling. He places his hands on his hips and gazes at the forest beyond, his eyes passing close to the spot where I am crouched. I barely dare to breathe. When he turns his head a little the other way, I raise the camera and take a photo of him. My heart thumping. Two men walk over to join him. One of them is talking loudly. The others *shhh* him to be quiet. While they're concentrating on each other, I take more photos, then I zip the camera into my trouser pocket. While my eyes are lowered, one of them shouts.

'*Bem ali!*'

My body turns to ice. I hear footsteps quickening to a run. More shouts. I don't want to move, but I must know if they're coming this way. I lift my head. They are on the far side of the clearing, heading away from me.

I take my chance. Crouching low, I retrace my steps towards the tree.

The door of a vehicle slams and there are more voices in the clearing. More men. Perhaps they will search the whole area again. A dog barks. If it picks up my scent, then no hollow in a tree can keep me safe.

I don't turn round. I start to run. Cramp sears through my calf muscle but I keep going. The men have trampled this way too, creating new tracks, making it hard to find the trail. Branches whip my face, leaves drag at my feet. I'm panting, my chest burning.

After a few minutes, I can't run any further. I pause with my hands on my knees, head dropped, trying to catch my breath.

I glance behind for the first time. There is no one following me. No one I can see.

I look at Mum's watch. The red line has finally moved, threading its way back along the route she took. Only with my footsteps.

She's in this forest. Somewhere. I will find her. I have to.

Right now, all I can do is retrace my steps to camp. But as I stare at the screen a bit longer, I see that someone else is there already, someone wearing my watch. Maria, or Pakoyai.

I hope with everything inside me that it's both of them.

Connect

I try not to limp, but cramp has made it impossible to straighten my leg. Limping requires twice the energy, and I have none. My clothes are soaked with sweat, and I'm covered in insect bites where the repellent has rubbed away. I have no water. It was in the rucksack, stuffed in the hollow of the tree.

I feel dizzy, as if the forest floor is swooping up to meet me. I've been walking for three or four hours, I'm sure. The camp can't be far away now, but I don't know how much longer I can keep going. I'm about to pause, to rest just for a moment, when a familiar smell mingles with the scent of earth and leaves. The smell of cooking. I lift my head and sniff the air. The smell is coming from somewhere up ahead.

I hobble towards it as quickly as I can. I don't care about the pain in my leg or the bites any more. The familiar shape of two ponchos strung side-by-side appears between the branches.

'Jackinho!' Pakoyai runs towards me. She throws her arms around me, then steps back, taking my arm and guiding me slowly to the swept clearing, as if I might break at any moment. Although I feel broken already.

'I thought you might be—I didn't know what had happened.'

Pakoyai fills a cup with water, then passes it to me, her brown eyes fixed on mine. 'I'm glad you're here,' she says.

I drink the water and hold out the cup for more. I barely have the strength to lift my hand.

'Where is Maria?' I whisper.

'Come.' Pakoyai walks towards the ponchos. When she sees that I am struggling to stand, she returns and takes my arm again.

I am too exhausted to feel curious. Everything feels strangely hazy, as if it's happening in slow motion.

Maria is by the edge of the poncho-tent.

'Jack,' she mutters softly as I enter. '*Graças a Deus.*'

She is thanking God, or the universe, or something, that I am safe. My eyes struggle to focus in the gloom, and then I see a shape in one of the middle hammocks. I edge closer.

Leaning over the shape, at the far end, is a man with bare shoulders and arms. He looks up. For a moment we hold each other's gaze and I realize that he's about the same age as me. Something about his confident, deliberate movements made him seem much older. He smiles, then lifts the poncho and disappears.

My eyes return to the shape. Somehow I know that it's Mum.

'She is sleeping,' says Maria.

I move nearer, holding the hammock to try and steady myself.

Her eyes are closed. The purplish shadows beneath make her face look so pale.

'Will she be OK?'

Maria nods. 'She's been shot in the leg. It was the loggers.' I feel the air leave my chest. 'The bleeding has stopped, but the bullet is still in there.'

'But is she just—sleeping?'

'She's had a natural sedative,' Maria whispers. 'When it wears off, she will be in a lot of pain. We need to get her to a hospital, fast, but I think she's going to be OK, Jack.'

A bandage has been wrapped around Mum's calf, held in place with palm leaves and twine.

'The boy you saw just now was the hunter. The one I met with Sofia. He risked his life to save her. The bullet struck her just below the knee. She managed to hide until morning but collapsed as she tried to walk back to camp. He found her. He stopped the bleeding and brought her here. He must have arrived a few hours after we'd left.'

I didn't even thank him.

An image of Dad appears in my head. An image I haven't allowed myself to look at, until now. He is lying in the hospital bed, hooked up to machines. He hadn't been ill. There was no warning. By the time I arrived, the doctors knew he wouldn't wake up.

I look at Mum, sleeping. I know that her eyes will open again, soon. I feel something which I thought I'd never feel again.

Lucky.

Hot tears rise up. I brush them away, but they don't stop.

Housebound

A door shuts, and my eyes flick open. There are no cicadas chirruping, no birds calling, no rustling or whooping. It's eerily still. I am lying on a sofa. I remember tumbling through the doorway yesterday evening, with barely enough energy to lift my feet. Pakoyai offering me her bedroom, which I refused. It wasn't fair to make her sleep on the sofa again. I see now why her walls are covered with paintings. Greens and reds and yellows, feathers and vines, bursting with sound and movement. I never imagined that I would miss the endless chatter of the rainforest. But I feel strangely boxed in, the ceiling too low.

I think back to my final few hours in the forest. Steering Mum's palm-leaf stretcher past vines and branches. Trying desperately not to bump her leg or snag her clothes on the grasping branches. Using our final reserves of energy to get her home before her wound became infected. Paulo was waiting for us in the inlet from where we'd set off, four days earlier. He used the motor to propel us downstream in half the time it took to travel up, slicing through the roiling water as fast as he could. Lucas drove us to the city, and straight to hospital. I wanted to go in with Mum, but she insisted that I went home to sleep. That there was nothing more I could do to help. I was so exhausted, I didn't argue.

I fold back the thin cotton sheet draped across my legs, then walk stiffly downstairs.

Maria is alone at the table, a half-eaten *tucuma*-cheese sandwich in one hand. She beckons with the other. It doesn't matter how softly I move, she always hears me coming.

'Jackinho,' she smiles, 'the nurse called last night. She said Sofia will be discharged this morning. The hospital is on the other side of the city, so I'm leaving early, before the traffic gets bad. I thought there was no point in waking you.'

I feel a buzz in my chest. 'I'll come too.' I picture the corridors, long and white. The smell of disinfectant. Dad.

Maria nods. 'Of course you can come, but there might be a lot of waiting around. I thought you should rest a little more, or get things ready here instead? There's a camp bed to set up, and Pakoyai will need help preparing a meal. I don't think the food in hospital is very tasty.'

'OK,' I agree. 'I'll get things ready.'

I still feel tired and weak, but I need something to keep me busy. Anyway, I'm not the one who was shot—except by a bullet ant, and I'm not sure that counts.

'*Obrigada.*' She stands up, draining the last of her drink. 'I'll be back in a couple of hours.'

A few minutes later, the front door clicks shut. Silence fills the house, pressing against the walls.

I pour myself a drink of water. A soft sound directly behind me makes me jump, and I splash water on the table.

'*Bom dia.* Sorry, Jack. Your hearing wasn't this good when you first arrived!' Pakoyai passes me a tea towel. 'Where's Maria?'

'Gone to the hospital.' Her eyes widen. 'Nothing bad. She's bringing Mum home. She asked me to stay and get things ready.' I point to the camp bed and pile of sheets.

Pakoyai takes some bread from a large basket.

I do the same. I sense that she is staring at me. My cheeks begin to burn.

'What?' I say, focusing on my piece of bread.

'That sketchbook in my room—it's yours?'

'Yes, just some—'

'I had a look inside. I hope you don't mind.'

I shake my head, wondering whether I do mind or not.

'It's really good. They're really—powerful.'

'Thanks. I like street art.'

'Street art?'

'Artwork on buildings—on the outside.' She frowns. 'Not graffiti exactly. Art which makes you look up, makes you think. It's actually really hard to have such a big... canvas, and make it look good.'

She nods, as if what I'm saying makes sense.

'I'm saving for a huge canvas.' Pakoyai holds her arms out wide, to show me how huge. 'Mum wants to know where I'll hang something that big, once it's finished.' She picks at her bread. 'Dad had a studio. That's what I want, when I leave school. A studio where I can paint and make artwork to sell.'

'Where is your dad now?' The question rushes out before I can stop it.

Pakoyai looks up from her bread, which is just

a pile of crumbs on her plate. 'He's been gone for eight years now.'

I watch Pakoyai, trying to figure what she means by 'gone'.

'He met Mum through her campaigning.'

'Campaigning?'

'Against illegal logging, protecting the rainforest. When he learnt about what had happened to my grandparents, he became an activist. Everyone knew who he was, but not everyone liked what he did. The people who made their money from poaching, from illegal logging, from mining. One day he was attacked on his way to the studio. He never came home. No one was ever arrested for the crime.'

I feel as if all the air has been sucked from the room. She is looking at me again, her brown eyes flicking around my face.

'How old were you?' I ask.

'Six. I was six years old. I find it hard, now, to think that he has been gone for more years than he was around.'

I feel tears pool in my eyes, but they're not for me. They are for Pakoyai.

'So you see, Jackinho, I know a bit about *saudade*.' She pauses. 'You need to hurry up and finish breakfast. That camp bed isn't going to put itself together.'

Heal

I hear Maria's key in the lock. Mum pushes through the doorway on a pair of crutches. Her face is pale, and she is frowning slightly. I can't tell if she's in pain, or the crutches are annoying her. Probably both.

'What took you so long?'

She looks at me for a few seconds. There's a strange kind of light in her eyes. 'Right. Not—poor Mum, I hope you're OK?'

I smile.

It's strange to see Mum struggling to get around. It's strange to see her struggle with anything. It's less surprising to notice she won't accept help. She waves a crutch at Pakoyai when she tries to steer Mum towards the table for lunch.

Maria has already told Mum what happened while she was missing, but after every mouthful she rests her fork on the plate, preparing another question for me—how did I find the hollow in the tree, where exactly was her headband? She wants to know how my leg feels, whether it hurts.

I have flashbacks to those moments near the loggers' clearing. To when they were pursuing Maria and Pakoyai. To the sounds of footfall outside the tree hollow. Explaining helps me make sense of what happened, to unravel the events balled-up in my head. But I still have questions. Questions for Mum.

Because Maria seems to think that Mum simply stumbled upon the loggers' clearing. That she was disorientated.

We have shared everything with Mum, now it's time for her to share with us. I don't want there to be any more secrets. They are like woodworm, eating away at anything solid. Anything good.

When there is a pause in the conversation. I can't wait any longer.

'What were you doing, so far from the trail?'

Mum glances around the table in surprise. Surely she's been expecting someone to ask?

'I strayed from the trail, Jack, I—' She seems about to explain, then stops. Her elbows rest on the edge of the table, fingertips pressed to her lips. She closes her eyes for a few seconds.

Maria pushes her chair back. 'Sofia? Are you OK?'

She nods, opening her eyes again.

'I'm sorry,' is all she says, shaking her head.

'Sorry for what? Sofia?' Maria asks, resting her knife and fork on the table.

'I wasn't lost,' Mum says. 'I'm sorry. I put you all at risk, and things could have ended far more badly than they did. I should have told you all what I planned to do.' She hesitates. 'I suppose I knew you'd try to stop me, and you would have had good reason.' She pauses again. 'Perhaps you've already guessed. I went to find the loggers.'

'*Sofia.*' Maria shakes her head.

'I wanted to film. I wanted some footage of them cutting down the trees. To show that they were in pristine forest. Untouched. That it wasn't an area designated for farming.' She rests her head in her hands. 'I put your people at risk, Maria, and all of you.' She glances round the table again. 'And for nothing. They saw me before I could take any pictures or film. I lost my camera.'

I put my glass on the table and stand up.

'Jack, I'm sorry,' Mum says quietly. But she has misunderstood.

234

Rather than waste time explaining, I run upstairs. When I return to the table a few minutes later, everyone is silent, still.

I place something on the table, next to Mum's hand.

She glances down, and gasps. 'Jack! Where—*how* did you get this?'

'You left it in the hollow of the tree with your watch. There are photos on there now. Good ones. None of them cutting trees down, but of the machinery and the clearing, of the truck piled up with logs. Number plates too. And faces.'

She sniffs.

'Jackinho! That was a very reckless thing you did. Very stupid!' says Maria. She runs around the table to hug me.

'Very brave,' whispers Pakoyai, tears sparkling in her eyes.

Mum switches on the camera and scrolls through some of the images, shaking her head.

'I can see their faces. I can identify them,' she mutters. 'Brilliant. *Brilliant.*'

'Later,' says Maria gently. 'Look later, Sofia.'

'There's a bag upstairs,' Mum says, her voice a little hoarse. 'My red bag, in Maria's room. Could you bring it down?'

As I head up the stairs again, Pakoyai's words echo round my head. *Very brave.*

The bag is wedged behind Mum's suitcase. I tug at the shoulder strap, wondering how I didn't notice something so brightly coloured on the flight out.

'Is this the one?' I place the bag on an empty chair next to Mum.

'Thank you.' She rummages around inside, pulling out a small parcel, which she hands to Maria, then another for Pakoyai. 'This is for you. *Feliz natal.*' She passes me a square package wrapped in singing-reindeer paper.

It feels heavy. Probably a book about space phenomena, or Egyptian tombs. At least, that's what she bought me last year, and the year before. I peel back a corner, arranging my face into a grateful smile of surprise. The paper falls away to reveal a book about graffitists, Cool Earl and Cornbread, and the history of street art.

I bend down to hug Mum.

'This is *so* cool!'

Pakoyai reaches out her hand.

'May I see?' She flicks slowly through. 'I *like* these,' she says. 'They're almost as good as yours.'

Mum looks at Maria. I feel my cheeks begin to burn again.

'There's another part to your present.' Mum clears her throat. 'I said I would try to get you home in two weeks. Well, the consultant said that I'm fit to fly. That means we can leave on the flight tomorrow evening. *Less* than two weeks.'

'That's great,' I hear myself saying, but the grateful smile—the real one—seems to have faded.

Fix

As I cross the road, wind nips at my face, numbing my cheeks. The school gates come into view. Dan is leaning against the wall, hands pushed deep inside his pockets. The knot in my stomach tightens. Ben appears, and they walk through the gate together. They haven't seen me. I could hang back, meet them in class. Instead, I speed up.

Before I can say hi, they stop in their tracks, staring—not at me, at something ahead.

I follow their gaze. Along one whole side of the science block, someone has sprayed *boring* in massive blue and white bubble letters. Zombie-like, we move closer. The letters are uneven and the paint has dripped where it's been sprayed too thickly. A crowd gathers either side, mouths hanging open.

'No. Way,' murmurs Ben.

'Mr Butler is going to go *ballistic*!' says Dan.

'Who would do something that *bad*?' I add. Although I know who.

'Hey,' Dan turns to face me, 'you're back.'

'Yeah,' I say,

'Good *trip*?'

'It was OK. How about you? Did Father Christmas bring that fire engine you asked for?'

He stares at me, frowning slightly, before a smile spreads slowly across his face. 'No, but I'm glad you got *razor-sharp wit* in your stocking.'

We head through the doors and into school.

The knot in my stomach doesn't go away, but I make it through the day.

I don't see Shiv or the others at break time or at lunchtime. I'm relieved. They might ask me what I think of the science block. They might ask me for the paint. I don't want them to have it. Not for something else like that.

When I get home, Mum is waiting in the kitchen, her leg propped on a cushion. She wants to know how my day went and I realize that I don't mind her asking.

'Jack,' she takes a small breath in, 'I've been going through the pile of post that was waiting when we got back. There's a letter from Ben's mum.'

'Ben's mum?' I ask, confused.

'She had a visit from a man who says he owns the art shop on the high street.' My heart skips in my chest. 'A group of boys went to his shop on their way home from school. One of them stole some items. He followed the group round the corner and saw them going into Ben's house. He'd captured an image of the thief on CCTV and showed Ben's mum the next day. She said it was clearly you, Jack.' Mum's eyes search my face, perhaps waiting for me to say it can't be true.

I feel the colour drain from my cheeks.

'I'm sorry,' is all I seem able to say. But I mean it.

'He hasn't been to the police yet. He wanted to talk to you first. But this letter is dated a few days ago. Perhaps it's too late.'

'I'll go now,' I say.

'*Now?*' asks Mum.

'If I don't go now, I might not go at all.'

'Well, fine, but I'm coming with you. You're under eighteen, Jack.' I think she expects me to protest, but I want her to come. 'I'm not sure I can walk far on those stupid crutch things. I'll book a taxi.'

When we arrive, it's almost closing time. I push open the door, and the bell tinkles. My mouth feels dry as I walk towards the till. I want to turn and run back through the door, to keep on running until I can't go any further. Instead, I approach the counter. The old man gets up from his chair.

'How can I help you?'

When I don't answer, he tilts his head to one side, squinting a little. 'Aren't you the boy—'

'Who stole from you. Yes.'

'Ah.' He nods. 'I didn't think you were going to come.'

'I'm sorry,' I say, placing some ten-pound notes on the counter in front of me. 'I hope that's enough.' I stare at the money, finding it hard to meet his eyes.

He pushes the notes towards me.

'I don't want your money,' he says. Now I look up, confused. 'That will make you feel better, and I don't want you to feel better. Not yet.'

I guess he's decided to go to the police after all.

'Have you stolen things before?' He looks at me through his bushy white eyebrows. I thought he wanted an apology. Now I'm not sure what he wants.

'No, that was the first time—and the last,' I add.

'I thought as much,' he murmurs. 'If I report you to the police, then you'll go to court. It won't be very nice for you or your mother.' He nods towards the door. 'You'll receive a fine, perhaps a note on your record, all your friends will know.' He rubs his chin.

'I thought I might give you a chance to show me that you've learnt your lesson first.' I stare at him, wondering what is coming next. 'I want you to *do* something to pay for it.' I wait for him to continue. 'That's it,' he says. 'I don't mean the washing up or putting the rubbish out. Something which takes time and effort. Then, when it's done, you can come and tell me about it.'

I turn to look at Mum. She raises her eyebrows.

My mind races. *Do* something? I have no idea what that could be, but this must be better than going to court.

'OK.' I nod slowly. 'Thanks...'

'Mr Kershaw,' he says. 'I believe it's harder to steal from someone once you know their name.'

That night, I lie in bed, staring towards the window as if an idea might blast through, on a gust of wintry air. I turn to face the door, tugging at my duvet which seems too big and too fluffy.

Doing something seemed like a brilliant deal at the time. Anything must be better than going to the police station. But what? My mind is blank. Maybe I could collect litter or help old people across the road.

It would have been so much easier to just give Mr Kershaw the money—or even the paint. I think he knew that. I shuffle to the edge of the bed and reach underneath. My fingertips brush the smooth cold surface of a paint can. Paint. Somewhere in my head, there is a kind of spark.

I throw my covers to one side and switch on the bedside light, sweeping away the clutter on my desk. I place my notebook in the space, and flick through to find a blank page. I begin to sketch.

Chance

'Jack!'

I open my eyes. I'm kneeling on the floor, my face resting on the bed. Beneath my cheek is something hard.

'Are you OK?' Mum is crouched down next to me.

'I had an idea,' I mutter, lifting my head.

'An idea?'

'For Mr Kershaw.' I yawn, pointing to the sketch-book which I'd been using as a pillow.

'School starts in twenty minutes, so we might need to talk about it later.'

'School is part of my idea,' I say, getting to my feet.

'So let me get this straight,' says Mr Willis, once everyone has left for home. 'You want to cover the graffiti on the side of the science block, with—more graffiti?'

'Not with graffiti, sir, with street art. I have some designs here.' I open my sketchbook and slide it across the desk towards him.

Mr Willis looks at me, one hand resting on my sketchbook. 'What makes you think the principal would even consider such a—such a wild idea?' he asks.

I shrug. 'It's really expensive to remove graffiti, and it doesn't usually all come off anyway.' He begins to turn the pages. Another thought pops into my head. 'Perhaps the design could change every year. Maybe there could be some kind of competition and—'

'Thank you, Jack. At this stage, let's just hope the principal finds time to look at your sketches.'

'You're going to show them to him?'

'I think it's worth a try. Yes.'

I walk slowly towards the gates. Most students have drifted home already. Dan is waiting by the wall.

'So?'

'He says he'll show the principal.'

Dan holds his hand in the air for a high-five. He's such a nerd, but I realize high-fiving is exactly what I want to do.

He heads home, and I wander down the street in the opposite direction. It's normally about now that the heaviness drifts down. For a while, I thought it had gone completely, but when I'm tired, or at the end of the day, I sense it hovering. It doesn't smother me like before. I know the feeling will pass.

Peace

'No, Jackinho!'

'She's booked flights.'

Pakoyai puts down her phone and runs around the room making whooping noises. There is a rustling-crackling sound as she scoops the phone up again.

'OK, well if you're coming so soon, there are things you should know. Mum has bought a sofa bed, so you can't moan about not sleeping. Oh, and we have a new first aid kit. It would be great if you didn't throw this one in the river.'

'What's that?' I point towards the wall behind her.

She grins. 'I finished it a few days ago. What do you think?'

'It's quite big.'

She gasps. 'Hypocrite!'

'OK, OK. Move a little closer. Hold the phone still.' She takes a few steps towards the wall and the enormous canvas, at least two metres wide. Huge leaves, in every shade of green, curve and sway round the edges. In the centre, a bird in vivid blues, reds and yellows stares defiantly back. It's vibrant, unsettling and beautiful.

'Not bad,' I say. 'Could the parrot be a bit bigger?'

'Arrrrgh!' She screeches with frustration.

'Come on,' I add, 'you know it's brilliant.'

She spins the phone back round. 'What's happened to your mural? Did you fix it?'

'Yeah, it wasn't too difficult. Annoying though.'

'Did they find out who sprayed over it?'

'They did actually. The headmaster installed some rapid-response security stuff, so when they returned, to spray over it a second time, the police arrived within a few minutes.'

'Who was it?'

'Four kids my age. They're going to be prosecuted.'

'Did you know them?'

'Yes, I knew them. Well, I thought I did, for a bit.'

She nods.

'I'm sorry, I've got to go—I'm finishing a piece of work, but can I call you at the weekend?'

'A piece of work for one of your *clients*?' She smiles.

'Some ideas for an infant school. They saw the design I painted on the science block. They want a mural for their library.'

'Sure, call me at the weekend.'

I place my phone on the desk, and stare through the window towards the house, breathing in the sweet pine smell. When Mum said I could turn the garden shed into a studio, I started planning before I'd even made it upstairs. I counted my savings. I had enough for a simple desk, a chair, a lamp and a small heater for winter. I used some old boards to make shelving.

Now I have my own space. Somewhere to draw. Somewhere to go when the whirlwind rises, although that happens less frequently.

Mum still works crazy hours, but she's around a lot more, and when she travels, I stay with Dan's family. His mum says one extra boy doesn't make much difference when she's already cooking a kilo of pasta for Dan and his brothers. Mum also agreed not to leave notes on the fridge. Message or talk is the rule. The talking part means no more secrets. Especially if she's planning to do something risky.

When the photos of the loggers were released, Mum got as much publicity as she could, but never mentioned Maria. They agreed it would be best if Mum was the public face, without compromising Maria's contacts. But that means Mum has to be extra careful whenever she visits. I like talking to her about it. It's also influenced some of the *important choices* I've made about which subjects I want to study.

In the shed, I think about Dad. A lot. I was worried about forgetting. Forgetting what he looked like, sounded like. Weirdly, the opposite has happened. I still have my favourite memories, but now they're mixed with others, featuring 'late' Dad or 'forgetful' Dad. Not always 'super' Dad. But always Dad.

I kept waiting to change back to old Jack, too, but things will never be how they were before. Pakoyai told me that when she first asked about her grandmother, Maria told her she'd had many names. That amongst her people, it's possible to choose a name to fit what is happening in your life. Her grandmother's final name meant *happiness*.

Without change, we'd all be like one of Mum's fossils. Gathering dust somewhere. Maybe missing out on some happiness.

Since meeting Pakoyai, I've realized there isn't one word in Mum's tattered blue dictionary which sums me up, and that whatever the future has in store for me, I will try to face it with courage. I also know that if courage fails me, there will always be someone who can lend me a little bit of theirs.

© Debra Hurford-Brown

ELE FOUNTAIN worked as an editor in children's publishing where she helped launch and nurture the careers of many prize-winning and bestselling authors. Ele's debut novel, *BOY 87*, won four awards and was nominated for ten more, including the Waterstones Children's Book Prize. She lives in Hampshire with her husband and two daughters.